The Feasting of Falerius

The Feasting of Falerius

DAVID GALVIN

DGP

MMIX

This edition first published in 2009 by
DGP
3 Burbage Road
Easton Royal, Wiltshire
SN9 5LT

A CIP catalogue record for this title is
Available from the British Library

ISBN 978-0-9563681-0-2

Typeset in Cycles at
Libanus Press, Marlborough

Printed in Great Britain by the
MPG Books Group, Bodmin and King's Lynn

The Feasting of Falerius

The potent mix of friendship, business and war
could lead to trouble …

A military and economic line has been drawn across the neck of Britannia by the emperor Hadrian and behind it, plough-teams of the wealthy take their agricultural riches from the island. Peace has brought prosperity and patrons with their clients settle down to meals of fine foods served in sumptuous rural villas: the economy thriving on its slave power.

Yet who were the slaves in this incessant desire for status and greed? Julianus Falerius Silvanus, a veteran soldier thought he had qualified to take his place at such a table but, lacking the social skills to survive, found himself being cheated out of his land by the elite that he could have died for. There were to be few appeals against corruption this far from Rome and it often drove men to take up the sword in anger. In this case, Attius, his son is left to complete the revenge.

LIST OF CHARACTERS

Julianus Falerius Silvanus (aka Falerius)   Ex-Centurion

Julia   Mother to Attius

Marcus Attius Octavianus (aka Attius)   Son of Falerius

Cominius   Serving army engineer

Marcus   Slave to Cominius

Longinus   Slave to Falerius

Gaius Helvius Bonus (aka Helvius)   Roman Magistrate

Cornix   Farm bailiff to Helvius

Tancorix   Slave to Helvius

Virius   Wool Merchant

Scribonius   Money Lender

Gaius Macrius Sulla   Legionary

Others

CONTENTS

Chapter I   The Homecoming

Chapter II   Men Who Built the Wall

Chapter III   Mercury's Hand

Chapter IV   Silver

Chapter V   On the Table

Chapter VI   Who to Trust

Chapter VII   Storms

Chapter VIII   Farewell Falerius

Chapter IX   Praise and Discipline

Chapter X   Gold

Chapter XI   A Decision to Run

Chapter XII   The Search for Attius

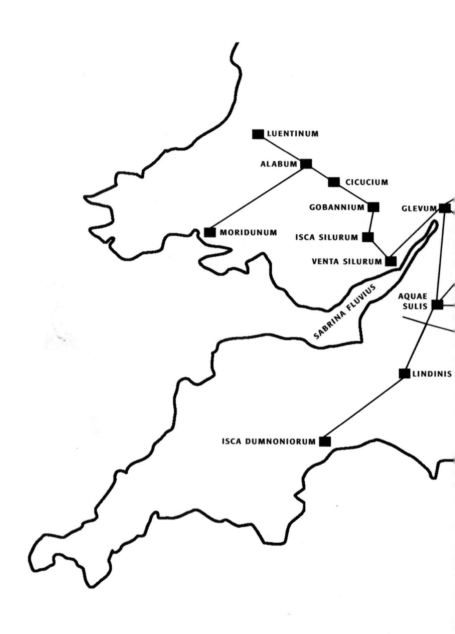

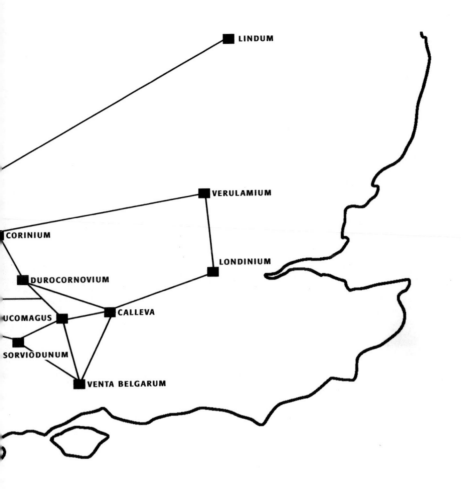

LINDUM

VERULAMIUM

CORINIUM

LONDINIUM

DUROCORNOVIUM

UCOMAGUS

CALLEVA

SORVIŌDUNUM

VENTA BELGARUM

ROADS & TOWNS OF
SOUTH-WEST BRITAIN
(not to scale)

CHAPTER I

THE HOMECOMING

January, and how much colder could it get? Across the vale, snow showers snaked their way smattering a thin dusting of white behind them and a winter's sun was growing weaker. Janus Clusivius had slammed the door of the old year shut and Janus Patulcius had prised open the lock of the new one to usher in an icy blast. Trees grouped as black cohorts of silhouette upon a blue horizon stood on immobile guard as snowflakes filed past in the breeze; the array of jagged wooden, spear-like limbs offering little resistance to the flesh of falling ice.

The old harvest of Ceres long past stuck its straw nails out of frozen furrows to snag the unwary. Sickly green and weak, the winter grass was weighed down, encrusted with a million droplets of frost. Sol would briefly illuminate all, tantalising the earth below by rippling his sunrays across the land and then disappearing in a grey shroud racing low from the icy north. Sheep heading for a hollow in the hillside cast no shadows in the late afternoon gloom and high on the ridge behind, the roman road from Calleva to Corinium ran silent, save for the necessary communication of Britannia conveyed by horsemen heads low down in the wind, their cloaks billowing out. Any news was not going to be quick in coming of the emperor Antoninus' plans.

Wisps of wood smoke from small farm villas were being washed into the huge columns of black emerging from the north. Storms were all around and to be indoors this day was wise. Hail thrown down indiscriminately beat against tiled roofs and then the noise would soften to a horizontal covering of snow as if the gods themselves had moved their hands and willed it. The white horse carving in the hillside that jutted out into the vale became neither chalk nor a horse. It became part of the landscape itself, the empty ditches of the fort guarding it quietly filling as the day wore on. How out of these few shortened hours of daylight, could fall whiteness so complete as to hide the paths of treacherous men? What gods had they on their side?

Marcus Attius Octavianus was such a man. He was a deserter, a thief and godless too having taken more time than he had wished to escape and return home. In order to fend off death Attius had become inured to stealing from shrines along the way just to eat, but this vale was his home and he had but a brief moment to return. In the few months of being away in the service of Rome, not much appeared different and under the blanket of snow, the prosperous land waited for Flora to herald the return of spring and exploitation to begin again. In these temperatures, the blood of the merchants was too thick for thought and the muscles of the slaves too tight for work. It required the warmth of longer days to see a better return. Yet Attius had not the time to wait. There were agents out looking for him and he was here for one thing and one thing only. That was to see death in the face of Gaius Helvius Bonus, the magistrate from Durocornovium.

With little to lose, Attius had long been frozen out. Pulling the prickly cloak tighter around his neck like a noose he shivered. He was standing in a small wood on the hillside, looking out, waiting for her to come. Somewhere a wolf called and his thoughts turned quickly to the amphitheatre, the last time an animal had served to chill his blood. With the ever-falling snow, he soon reverted to crouching low on his haunches, the cloak hanging like the military tent around his frame. It was getting late. His head throbbed as if there was a wrestler's hold around it and the swirling snowflakes served to blur his vision. He felt increasingly nauseous. With little warmth in his body, his fingers became claw like and shaking.

'Attius . . .' Her voice was slightly louder than that of the wind. 'Attius, is it you?' A pale shrouded figure spoke.

'Mother!' He stood up straight as best he could and watched her walk cautiously towards him through the hindrance of the storm 'Who have you there?' Attius asked, knowing that he had knowledge of the emperor.

'It's alright, you can trust him. It is Cornix, the bailiff of that evil dog

Bonus. There are animals out here that have not killed or eaten for many a day. I needed to bring the safety of another.'

Attius reached out and touched her face desperately seeking warmth, and then embraced. Despite his ordeals, she had taken the risk and come. 'My coded message, you understood?' He whispered.

'Yes.' She replied.

The long months slowly fell away like loaded dice falling from a game of chance and revealing the truth. It hurt to remember the sadness of being forced to leave home, the death of his father, that also of Longinus, the loss of the land, the misery of the army and of that bastard Gaius Helvius Bonus.

'Where is he mother? Is he there?' Her son hissed and gestured towards a tiny speck in the valley below two miles distant. Even in the darkened hours, he still knew where his enemy was.

'He is, and he knows little or nothing. Due to the cold, there has been a suspension of business in Durocornovium and since, he has been drinking heavily at home. He does not know where you are and stopped asking long ago. We will need to go quickly.' The tiny group slid into the darkness of the valley below led by Cornix, the slave bailiff who had first hand knowledge of the roman ways of justice. As he had no rights then Bonus had no right to his loyalty, with every poor master having to count the knives in his kitchen.

The path to the bottom of the hill was difficult to negotiate. The lateness of the afternoon hour and the brown of the wood without vegetation conspired to make it appear impassable. Underfoot it was slippery. Attius' boots had long lost their hobnail teeth from their soles thus giving little bite. Cornix slithered about in a pair of cheap indoor sandals and Julia, daintily trying to avoid falling over, went from branch to branch across the path. It wasn't like this for Attius as a boy. He remembered the day winter broke out into spring. The ponies racing up this track to carry him and Longinus to the hill fort above. Roman versus Celt; the old battles and the old ways. They were natural enemies where often only the Celtic ancient pagan spirit survived, the flesh torn apart by repeated contact with the legions. A tear, brought on by the cold if anybody had asked, started to well up in Attius' eye but was met by the steely urgency of revenge and dried. There was never going to be any other way than this and the lead curse seals of hatred had been slowly unfurling in his mind revealing their purpose.

The chained guard dog in the villa's compound met them with an aggressive warning but was easily soothed by Cornix who put him away. Across the cobbled courtyard, the pebbles shone through where a repeated effort had been made to get to the wood store and back. Through the snow, they resembled the frozen knuckles of the dead slowly buried by a drifting white ash. A dim light burnt through the door cracks of the villa's main room. The corridor wings of the building housing the bedrooms and kitchen were dark, and high behind the villa itself the protective hills slipped into the night. Within five miles or so, few lights flickered or could be seen.

'Cornix, go indoors and make sure that he has no guests. Check the bedrooms.' Attius whispered, 'Mother you go too.'

Cornix and Julia disappeared through a side door into one of the wings and, after what seemed ages, raised voices were heard. A pot smashed and the main door opened through which Cornix found himself being thrown landing hard upon the courtyard surface. He picked himself up and crept low towards Attius hiding in the relative safety of the outbuilding.

'Well?' Attius enquired urgently.

'He's been on his own all day since we left and is heading towards being drunk,' Cornix spat. 'Nobody has cooked for him and he has an empty stomach of cold food. There is nobody else with him and the only warm room is the dining room. He is in a rage having had to keep the brazier going all afternoon and wants to know where we have been. He wishes also that he were back in his town house with all its comforts even though he couldn't be seen to drink as he does here. Since your leaving, he has done little except ruin us all in body and steal what was your father's. This farm is nothing to him and I too would wish him dead.'

Attius knew the penalties for Cornix thinking like that. The only resolution was going to be the certainty of death and for him that was the same. A roman citizen murdering a roman citizen – there would be repercussions upon his family and property. Bonus had to be seen to meet with a natural end. Attius ordered Cornix to remain where he was before approaching the wooden main door to the villa. Through it, he could hear his mother's voice trying to explain her absence for the latter part of the day. He put his hand slowly on the latch and felt the ironwork through his fingers. It had been forged from a spear point that had once wounded his father and which he had kept. A memory silently returned and faded. He opened the door gently and slipped inside closing it behind him.

Bonus, propping himself up on a couch, had his back to him with his mother standing facing the door through which Attius had crept. A small clay beaker of beer stood on a low wooden table along with the profit and loss ledgers of the business. An iron brazier burnt slowly in the corner casting its warmth over the painted plaster walls and the simple geometric design of the mosaic floor. Scraps of food lay in shallow grey bowls on a wooden table. The shutters in the windows were fighting to keep the warmth in and the clay tiles on the shallow roof rattling with the wind. In the corners of the room, there were two doors to the kitchen and bedrooms. The little household shrine behind the door was standing protector over all within.

'What's up with you woman?' slurred Helvius Bonus. 'Have you cast eyes upon Vesta herself?' he mocked.

'No, I see my son,' she simply replied.

'What stupid nonsense you are talking! He left, remember, or more to the point he had to leave.' Bonus sniggered. 'The dead cannot return. Now fetch me some food and where is Cornix?'

Bonus rose from the couch and addressed his scruffy appearance. Beer stained his tunic and crumbs of food stuck to his bulging stomach. He shook himself clean as if waving away petitions and turned for the door.

'By the Gods! Who are you? Julia, get Cornix and the dog,' he screeched. 'What do you want with us?'

Attius lunged for his throat wanting to hold him tight whilst he looked into his eyes, both hands gripping him for dear life. About the room, oil lamps flickered in the commotion and shadows played over the painted walls. Attius' face loomed close. He had a weathered sallow complexion with cold eyes and a heart to match. A deep burn scar was nearly hidden in the filth and daily grime of his beard. Bonus quickly realising the fight was useless relaxed into bargaining for his life, his body becoming a dead weight in his enemy's hands.

'What have you come for? Are you in trouble? I can help. Let me help you! I am your friend remember. Do you remember?' Bonus grovelled. 'Julia,' he whimpered, 'Please help me. Please, please spare me, both of you.'

Attius couldn't. He looked at the magistrate and hated all that he saw. Here was the weaker man that followed every army with his selfish laws for a sword. The weaker man that gladly talked of others dying for him and the weaker man that fed off suffering and then grew strong. Instinctively his right hand felt for the sword pommel at his side and in a second, it was free of its scabbard. Mars Ultor, Mars the Avenger stood silently proud in relief decoration upon the leather bound sheath watching the unfolding event. Punching Bonus hard in the stomach, Attius drove the sword home. Gaius Helvius Bonus fell from his grip and clutched at the wound. He briefly gurgled spitting flecks of blood across the floor before slipping away to join the ranks of the damned on the banks of the River Styx. It was over and Attius felt sick and empty. It hadn't been the right ending.

'It is finished mother,' he said without apology for what she had to witness. 'My father has had his say and now we must plan to escape; fetch Cornix in.' Julia left the room returning quickly with the slave. He wasn't sad to see Bonus' prostrate body lying on the floor and in equal measure Cornix swung his foot hard into the dead man's back. 'Take his legs,' and Attius gestured, 'I'll carry his head', the two of them carrying the useless limp body out into the dark cobbled yard.

'Cornix, open the dog's door,' the slave doing as he was ordered. The still warm body was thrown in and the animal swiftly moved to sniff his meal. 'We'll let him feast tonight to make it look like a wolf attack and then leave his body in the woods. If the fates are with us then the snow will melt and hide our tracks. For tonight we all need to rest. Come and bolt the door.'

Through sleep the wheel of life revolved. The vengeful Diana in the guise of the moon gave way to Apollo in the morning sky and the time for vindictive actions had ended. The hunter had struck home.

In the early morning light Attius and Cornix carried the lifeless body of Bonus to where the spring feeding the villa bubbled from beneath the hills. It was a short walk and for many a year fresh clean water had been provided by the Earth Goddess. This was to be her sacrifice, her reward. Bonus' lifeless body slid down the bank and landed at an accidental angle in the bottom of the ditch. It could have been so. A drink indoors and then a noise outside; your torch is blown out and you slip. No one hears from you again.

That done they returned to the small villa where Julia was busying herself. The fire in the brazier was relit, the blood scoured from the mosaic tiles by greensand and water, and an earthen pot of barley porridge popped on the fire grate in the kitchen.

'Cornix, put the dog away. Scrape up the snow in its cage and carry it to the stream. Let it melt away and then come back. We'll keep the food warm for you.' Attius went indoors.

The shutters were open to allow in the light through broken poor glass panes. Outside appeared as a confusion of white and brilliant blue sky. It was difficult distinguishing the facts of where something started and where it had ended. Inside however it was different with Julia having cleaned thoroughly, Cornix still working outside. With everybody sleeping badly last night there was a rush to conclude business and leave. However the more they hurried the longer it took and Attius worried that the snow stopping would bring visitors to the villa. Julia comforted him by saying that only dark smoke would attract anybody's attention and if he could, only to burn the driest of logs. A horse ride from Durocornovium was in the order of an hour or two and as the villa possessed meagre stabling then visitors would often leave the same day. Those who ventured out often did so in the warmer months when travel was safer and the animals left out in the paddocks. Since the villa lacked a bathhouse then guests could not expect opulent comfort prior to dining and enjoy the chance of scraping themselves clean. Hidden from the nearest arterial road it rarely received unwanted visitors.

Attius and his mother ate in silence. Hard cheese and stale bread to finish and a drop of sweet wine from blue glass beakers warmed them. Julia was the first to break the silence. 'You have yet to tell me what's happened to you. Since your father's death I had little choice in matters and Bonus . . . well he was there.'

'Mother I understand,' he interrupted. There was the shame at first and then a dawning reality that everything in life is preordained with a god for everything. Men's actions are governed elsewhere and control fickle. If they were to be cursed then so be it.

'Mother, Longinus . . . he is . . .'

'He is what, son?' She knew that he was dead.

The door opened and Cornix entered. A bowl was passed to him from which he ate gratefully. Their brief conversation ended all too suddenly like a candle snuffed out of its own accord and Attius, keen to be away but wanting to pay his respects to his father, went off alone. Julia understood.

The graveyard to the villa contained one grave, that of Julianus Falerius Silvanus. A tall simple wooden block stood erect in the chalk and greensand landscape, snow having gathered on the northern side. On its split niche was carved a simple family group standing behind a reclining figure on a couch. All faces staring blankly out. Before the reclining figure a bench and some paperwork lay. The painted tunics of the family and the deceased had not yet weathered completely and looked bright and cheerful in the winter sun. In the panel below was detailed Falerius' life.

D · M

J · FALERIVS · G · F · GALERIA · LVGDVNI
SILVANUS · C · LEG II AVG ·
ANNORVM DXII STIP XXV HEREDES FECIT CVRAVERVNT

H S E

To the Spirits of the departed

Julianus Falerius Silvanus · Son of Gaius from the voting tribe of
Galerians from Lugudunum · Centurion Second Augustan Legion
52 years of age served 25
His heirs had this erected

Here he lies

At the same time, it said everything and said nothing. The figure on the couch wasn't Attius' father. It was a roman made up in the roman way. Yet for Attius there was a strong need to be here kneeling on the frozen ground.

'Father, it is your son speaking. Are you still near or has your spirit long left for Hades? That gutless coward Helvius Bonus stares out from the banks of the Styx as Charon gloriously rows you across the river. Are you to join the brave fallen souls and walk amongst the best of men? Father I have come to remember you,' he whispered.

Attius knew that since his father's death he hadn't been back. The festival of the dead family member, the Parentalia was in February. Could he make amends now? In a small leather pouch he had brought pieces of cake and a drop of wine in a glass bottle. Firstly, there was work to be done. With cold hands, he scooped away the accumulation of snow at the base of the tombstone remembering well the day they interred his father's ashes. He knew also of the grave goods, the food and drink supplied to prevent the dead spirits from roaming above the grave in search of sustenance from the living. It was to be a long journey that of the dead. Into the frozen grass, he made a square cut and lifted out the turf putting it to one side. With the blade, he scraped at the cold clammy earth scooping it out with rigid fingers and piling it up carefully. After a while, he struck a pot and picked at the soil around its sides. He cupped it in his hands and pulled gently as it broke away from the freezing grasp of soil and felt heavy. There was nobody about.

Attius prepared to empty his find and tilted the pot upside down; he tapped it with the knife handle and then shook it for good measure. In seconds, the silver goods fell into the snow. On the grass lay 500 or so silver denarii none yet blackened by age. They were true solid coins of good metal and bore the portraits of strong emperors. The propaganda still spoke after all these years. This was Falerius' legacy to his son and the one the earth could never steal from him.

He uttered a brief prayer and gave thanks before restoring the ground. In knowing that he wouldn't ever be coming back, he crumbled the cake in his fingers and let it fall to the earth. Attius then withdrew the cork stopper from the bottle and poured a libation into the snow allowing it to seep into where the money had come from. 'Father, journey safely. May we meet again.' With his heart heavy Attius picked up his legacy and left.

Why would Pluto of the Underworld take living men's spirits and return them to the shadows amongst waving trees? Attius felt there was nobody to answer his question and that the gods or goddesses of this place weren't listening either.

CHAPTER II
MEN WHO BUILT THE WALL

It was eight hundred and eighty one years after the founding of Rome that the legionary fortress of Isca in western Britannia made preparations to greet more of its soldiers, the Second Augusta, home. The fort, quietly nestled in its river valley and surrounded by the once hostile mountains of Siluria, had changed vastly. Wooden structures had been replaced by the more permanent stone and like lichen a small settlement attached itself to the outside face of the stark monument to roman military power. Occasionally the wooden gates would spew out a select cohort of soldiers together with their superior weaponry and, in a rush of colour and noise they would be gone; an uprising in the remoter mountain villages, an outpost attacked, a convoy ransacked or a road to build. The settled veterans would remember it all too well. The pump of blood, the shake of muscles and having to trust the old legion to defend them. Tales of past bravery would be mixed with hidden fears of the future. Not all of Britannia had been subdued and, beneath the veneer of these roman ways of life, a fire still burnt in the Celtic world for freedom. Mocking tales were often heard of remote tribesman having no need for money, not wishing to live a better life in the few towns that struggled for existence or wanting to learn the new language of the Romans. It mattered nothing to them.

Early on a warm and bright September morning, twenty miles or so from Isca Silurum, one of those vexillations of Roman soldiers readied itself for the last stage in its long march from the north. They hadn't been on the routine patrol duty reserved for others. They had been engaged in the hard physical labour of building the wall of Hadrian from sea to sea. Solid and strong it stood as the symbol of permanence and built by human flesh without the divine intervention of gods or giants. Stoutly it looked out over the northern valleys and forests rearing up against anybody wishing to challenge the might of Rome itself. Once soldiers had campaigned beyond it, yet the empire didn't require wastelands or hard to win wealth any more and military glory was a distant memory held within the books of the educated. The Second Augusta was to be locked away along with the other two legions of Britannia, and the key to the province's security given to their auxiliaries. To the men waking up that morning and all throughout the march home it was a time of reflection and uncertainty. What was coming next?

With breakfast prepared and eaten the leather tents, the papilio, were taken down, rolled up and tied onto the carrying frames on the mules' backs. Overnight fires were snuffed out by hairy legged, sandal wearing legionaries who shook their woollen tunic shoulders to fit comfortably into the iron cuirass segmentata their colleagues were unselfishly fitting on their backs and tying. Nobody spoke. Other belongings, which were few on campaign, were stashed away on the mule except money, which was carried by the untrusting soldiers themselves in small leather pouches. One by one nearly a thousand men readied themselves and joined those already leaning on their spears and large shields, scratching patterns in the dust with the soles of their boots. It was still early morning, the grass damp, and the evidence of an overnight stay lay all around in the form of dry patches on the ground where the tents had been. In miniature it resembled the far larger permanent fortress and the design had not been coincidental. In a night attack upon the camp all soldiers knew where to assemble best to fight the enemy off; but this was friendly territory long fought over by the legions and hard won by them.

A slight breeze gifted by Aeolus blew up and the standards fluttered; the Capricorn rippling across the cloth vexillum. For soldiers without their helmets on, it was a cooling face wash. Six men trying to sleep in a tent and being disturbed by two others changing guard duty during the night was difficult. Some snored, all stinking of wood smoke and iron, whilst others couldn't sleep because of their fears and superstitions. Yet there they stood day after day brought together by a fierce bond of loyalty and discipline. The lack of deserters was a pride unto themselves.

The baggage train mules were coerced into position at the rear, along with the motley array of camp followers living off the army's fortunes and, without discipline they were to take much longer to ready themselves and therefore risk being left behind. Around loitered the cavalry escorts, some saddled up and ready, some returning from early reconnoitring, others setting fire to the temporary thorn stockades that had sufficed for protection the previous night. The smoke from these fires in attempting to rise fell back to earth and rolled across the fields with the wind. Horses and men fidgeted, all keen to be off. The September weather was good for marching, cool and clear and with the sun up the message was given for all to fall in and be quiet. After being raised high, the cohort standards once more pointed the way and the cornicens sounded a low note that rent the morning air with a reminder that Rome still ruled here. Different accents amongst the ranks, different languages, now obeyed the Latin commands barked down the rows and rows of soldiers. Auxiliary cavalrymen leaping into their saddles snatched up their reins. Long oval shields hung from their sides and their legs swayed with their horse in a saddle without stirrups. Looking down they could see the silver iron helmets of the legionaries below them; no two necessarily the same design. They watched as their comrades shuffled into readiness, the shields being drawn up and their spears sloped across their shoulders. Ahead lay the road.

'Milites. Intente!'

At the head of the column was the tribune. He fussed over his orders and was wise to do so. His superiors had given him the responsibility of getting the vexillation home safely and the lesser troops below him looked up to a commander who was decisive and didn't unnecessarily risk their lives. Fortuna could be fickle in her dealings and rather than try to recover or hide a loss, it made military sense to prepare well and save luck for the battlefield where it may be needed most. They had lost men recently but mainly through illness or deserted in search of better food.

They were still after all only on the edge of Siluria and the mountains held a refuge for the bravest prepared to come out and fight the smaller legionary force. Today though it was quiet and the only real enemy to be found was a callous on the foot or a tight muscle. Every man's thoughts stretched ahead the twenty miles to the bath house in the fortress and his bunk to sleep in.

The tribune finely accoutred in his cuirass and his splendid helmet nodded to the horn bearers, and the large round brass instruments gave sound to the march. In full order the column lurched forward. The horizon swayed before them and the crunch of military hobnails rang upon the road surface. Soldiers jangled as their iron plated armour slid over itself and clanked. Nearly a thousand spear tips scratched at the sky and on the left side a vast wall of leather clad shields seemed impregnable as it edged along. The military was on the move.

Beside the road jogged the cavalry, chain mail rippling over their sides, shields idly hung over their shoulders and their long swords bouncing against their right thigh. On their harnesses hung the good luck pendants, the masculine sun and the feminine moon. Their helmets adorned with a yellow horse hair crest hid their faces behind cheek pieces and their sandaled feet were working hard on the horses' bellies to discourage the slow. The occasional beast would rally against it all, the horns, the soldiers, the noise and result in that particular soldier falling out of place and retiring to a safe distance much to the mirth of all. The banter was exchanged until silenced by the Optio's stick across a soldier's back. Although it was one empire with many legions there were still deep differences within them and a cavalryman would always say that it was better to ride than walk. An infantryman would reply that he wasn't paying to feed two mouths.

In stages along the road, and the closer to Isca, the order was given to relax. The standards were lowered and carried across the shoulders of their bearers yet the speed of the march maintained by the military pace. Occasionally country dwellers would stop their work in the fields and gaze at the soldiers. Here they were used to roman intrusion, the comings and goings of units of the army but weren't afraid. The might of Rome passed by – all the wood, leather, iron and horse flesh bound up in the spirit of man. The emperor's soldiers all doing what the emperor wanted. Even in Britannia, the province where honest men could never become truly rich a strong army presence was still required and there was no leaving now. The prosperous Roman Empire was being allowed to grow and develop under the emperor Hadrian, and Britannia, the backwater that it was had to pay its way. Keeping an army was expensive in taxes and taxes had to come from the land. The land advance however was now enclosed within a wall – Hadrian's, and the armies enclosed within their forts.

From the agger of the road, Centurion Julianus Falerius Silvanus, looked down upon the labourers. They very quickly went about their business. The September harvest of barley and wheat was there to be won. Whilst the military presence brought them peace it also brought resentment for agricultural land close to a large fortress was ripe for redistribution amongst retiring veterans of the legion. The best land was acquired not for the best price and the occupants moved away to farm the less productive plots. It seemed that the land was everything and to have a large estate, with a large villa the ambition of all. Yet few ever made it that far. Falerius watched as the Celts scratched the earth with their ploughs and broke their backs to cut the corn. The golden harvest silently going on as far away men fought over fewer riches; savage men of the north, wanting to steal the wealth of others. He had fought men that he couldn't see; an enemy so quiet that even the wind through the short thin stalks of barley would conceal an arrow shot. Yet to some this was victory. This was the opportunity to carve a military career in winning vast tracts of useless land, killing barbaric people in the name of Rome. He had seen good friends die in a place not of their choosing, alone and afraid and deserted by their mighty gods. He had seen the wounded left whilst the remaining threw down their arms and ran away. The military conquest was always recorded in great battles not in the day to day struggle for survival in a remote and inhospitable land. He had gone into battle himself with hope and left with despair. Looking down from the road he understood it all. Would he have the strength to fight his demons in the shady quiet backwater of a farm? This was the life that he had planned with Julia and their son. Take the money, take the land and turn his sword into a plough.

Falerius looked at his century of men, depleted and awaiting reinforcement. Most were known to him, the cowards and the brave. Some were marching with a slight limp, others shuffling the weight on their shoulders attempting to hide a silent injury crying out in pain. Nobody wanted to be cast out and discharged without their due reward. The army paid you, fed you and kept you well whilst your friends looked after you. The last mile or so was a march to safety and in the back of their minds they all knew that far away others were now fighting for their lives. Some of his century would die of their wounds once back, others forced to leave the safety of the fort and live out their lives clinging to the fortress walls in a hovel. The strong and the experienced would be retained until released. There were new recruits to train up as they began their probatio and what better man than one who has seen it all. Falerius knew that he would be kept by the army yet that suited him. The campaigning season was coming to an end and any local warlike tendencies or insurrections were often secondary to bringing in a harvest with which to pay your taxes and to survive through the winter. He had nowhere to go and although safe and warm within the fortress throughout the oncoming autumn and winter months he knew that Julia would be comfortable and close by in the settlement outside the walls. Moreover it gave them time to plan for their future.

Falerius couldn't look at the slaves anymore in the field. In his way he had helped to put them there and wondered about his own impending enslavement to the land. For the time being though he had to take what was to be offered to him and in pushing himself a little harder he urged the others to do the same for the end was close now.

An hour later a cavalry rider approached. The many gravestones along the roadside bore testament to more civilization. They were well clear of the long open fields now and instead small allotments parcelled the land up. To the south west Falerius could see above the orange tiled roofs the stone battlements of the fortress. An order was given and the column stopped. The military pace was changed into a parade order; soldiers shuffling into their precise lines. The centuries with their centurions, the cohort standard bearers, the tribune and the cavalry escort all in place. From the cemetery the dead looked impassively out upon the scene their limestone relief faces coldly inspecting the line of soldiers. The dead exploits detailed in fading bold red paint in a panel beneath: died aged thirty, centurion of fifteen years service, from Gaul, from Germania. They were all far from home. The delicately carved insignia were instantly recognisable. This legion, that cohort, all now silent and all now gone. A few people fussing over a grave turned to look at the new arrivals. Word was about that they were returning home but nobody knew how many or who was still alive, for they had been away for many years. Life could often be short. As the standards were raised for the last time the onlookers came closer to the road accompanied by others coming out from their shops that fronted the street. They came a lot closer than the country dwellers who had chosen to keep their distance. A line of cheering faces greeted the soldiers as they marched on towards the river crossing and the parade ground on the other side. Falerius' heart beat a little faster now, his muscles felt a little stronger and his pride grew a little greater. This was the end.

The vexillation were directed to the parade ground that lay to the northwest of the fortress and alongside the amphitheatre. Here a role call was taken and the strength of the returning force established by the tribune and the centurions. The cavalry horses too tired to worry about anything stood motionless, their riders stiff in the saddle and keen to dismount. There was to be no overnight temporary camp tonight;

instead soldiers would sleep safely behind walls built of stone safe in the knowledge that they weren't going to fall asleep on duty and be caught out doing so. Instead of grass for a bed there would be straw. Instead of sleeping with one eye open, others would be watching over them.

As the centuries were called out one by one, they picked up their shields in their left hands, sloped their spears over already tired shoulders and marched triumphantly through the western gate and then dispersed into their barrack blocks, the same eight men to a room as in the tents. The order came for the horsemen to get down from the Magister Equitum, and after sliding off, shields across their backs, they attempted to stand up straight again under the weight of the chain mail. The riders then gathered up their reins and led the weary beasts to the stables also inside the fort. The standard bearers along with the musicians walked solemnly behind the mounted tribune to the Principia building half way along the Via Principalis, one of the three main streets that crossed the fort at right angles meeting in the centre. Here they were met by the Praefectus Castrorum, the second in command deputising for the legionary Legate who was away on other business. Seeing they were tired he kept his speech short and thanked Fortuna upon their collective behalf for bringing them safely home. The standards with due reverence were then returned to the safety of the sacellum and the pay chest of the cohorts locked away. The animal skins of the cornices and vexillarii, the wolf and bear skins were then carefully removed and hung to one side.

The day was getting later, too late for the bath house to operate, their furnaces allowed to die down ready for rekindling the following morning. However activity swarmed about. Now free of their armour and the discipline of march, the soldiers sought out old comrades, themselves back from the north, whilst others prepared the evening meals in the ovens built into the revetments inside the wall. Cavalrymen still with their mounts cleaned them down, as the less encumbered donned tunic and cloak to seek out the pleasures outside the walls, usually a cup of beer and a prostitute. Past them barged fresh horsemen sent out to accompany the baggage train safely home whilst behind in a green sky rose the noise of success. Even the wizened old guards on the walls were smiling for they knew that in a day's time military discipline would be back with a vengeance.

Falerius' thoughts turned to Julia. He had a slave go into the vicus and rent a room for her and their son. The slave was also to wait until the baggage train arrived and make her comfortable. There was little more that he could do as the tents and military equipment travelled at their own speed. Falerius instead stalked off looking for his century and their barracks. They were on the northern side of the fort and at the end of the row of tiny eight man rooms was his own, a little larger, more private and more comfortable. In the corner a brazier had been lit and the charcoal lumps glowed quietly as Falerius opened the door. On a table lay a simple supper of warm pork cooked in cumin, cheese and bread. A jug of watered wine had also been left with a small samian cup to drink from. Oil lamps left a sooty trail in the warm clammy air providing just enough in the way of light. For Falerius it was his room and he had fought hard to earn the privilege however meagre and, as a slave began to unbuckle his armour, his thoughts began to peel away with it. He was going to miss this life as it had been all he had known. The dangers, the travels, the adventures and of course the financial rewards which hadn't been insubstantial. Could he walk behind a plough in the fields anymore than he could sulk behind the recruits as an instructor? With his armour off he felt a new freedom and with cupped hands washed the aches out of his shoulders from a bucket of cold water. He was now forty three years of age. His body had borne the brunt of battle, long cold nights on the ground, the exertions to risk running away from for some, and the rare indulgences of female company. He had given his life for the army, seen others give theirs and wanted to reap his rewards from the new peace imposed by Hadrian. The new wall from coast to coast, the three legions, all the auxiliaries and cavalrymen too. In his mind he tried to count them all and in doing so very quickly fell asleep on his bed.

A gentle shake on both shoulders woke him. 'Centurion Falerius, you asked me to wake you. There is a meeting of all officers of cohorts V and VII in the Principia.' Through the small window autumn shone in a rectangular block of white light upon the plastered wall. The brazier, barely warm sent up specks of dust in the commotion of his rising and getting dressed. Last night's evening meal lay on the table largely unnoticed. A fresh selection of apples and hedgerow fruit looked more appetising set in a small round shallow samian bowl. He clutched at the blackberries and enjoyed the sweet cleansing taste in his mouth. A large crunching bite into an apple further helped to polish his breath. He was ready and closed his room behind him to walk the short distance to the headquarters building. There the other centurions and standards had gathered. The meeting was brief. There were to be two days of rest for those returning from the north without exertion or training. However fatigues still had to be assigned to the men. After two days the cohort's strength would have been assessed and new recruits sent to start the process of blending in with their new comrades. Damaged equipment was to be repaired, the sick to seek necessary help and normal garrison duties were to resume. The Praefectus Castrorum was keen to maintain a fighting legion despite the emperor having now ordered them home. The ebb and flow of seasonal campaigning, April to September, with its losses and gains was drying up. With it the glory that was truly Rome had found the limit of its expansion upon the furthest slopes of Britannia. Battle honours would be hard to win and sacred Jupiter's eagle's wings cupped in the mortal hands of man.

A selection of men were called out and asked to remain behind. These were the veterans, Falerius included, whose service was coming to an end. Since they were no longer at war the emperor had little need for them and the camp commander added that the duty of protecting the province had now fallen on the mixed cohorts of auxiliaries. However, since it would take time for the tessarius to complete his records of discharge, they were all welcome to remain in service until the spring.

He could use their knowledge on the training grounds and, importantly the centurions were encouraged to name their men as their replacements for promotion. The meeting over all dispersed into the pleasant hazy warmth of a new morning where Sol was struggling to look down upon the face of man.

Falerius made for the shrine of Fortuna where he cheekily offered up a little of last night's food and prayed for the future. Was anybody there? He thought it better not to cross the boundary of knowing more than the gods and after all he had arrived home safely. That part of the day completed he left to find Julia, having spoken the password quietly to the guard on the southern gate.

Activity outside the fort was brisk. New soldiers, deprived for so long of comforts were easy pickings. Meats and vegetables abounded at this prosperous time with market traders doing a good business. With the military restriction of eating only twice a day on campaigns lifted, the troops enjoyed all that was on offer and, what's more, they had another day to come in relaxing too. A short distance away was the town of Venta Silurum where your money could buy you anything from a soothsayer to a masseur to a jeweller.

Julia's room was as he had asked. Two beds, regular meals and privacy. He slipped a few more coins into the hands of the landlord, a veteran himself, and agreed that they would be requiring the room for the fore-seeable future – spring at the earliest and, providing Falerius didn't drop dead, this was a ready income; the deal was easily sealed. With the door quietly closed the pair of them began the slow process of being together again without the army, their discipline or the rigours of moving to and fro. In the corner slept Attius. He had ridden most of the way south in the back of a cart laden with belongings from all over, Julia had walked. Without hobnails in her shoes she had worn out four pairs and joked that every time that she saw the backside of the oxen all she could see before her were more shoes. Falerius comforted her promising that he would get a few more pairs made by a leather working friend of his.

The morning passed in quiet pursuits and Falerius stayed for most of the afternoon, playing with the boy when he awoke. Outside his military duties he promised to see them every day and assured Julia that the end of his time in the army wasn't too far away. She was pleased, Falerius unsure. He would have his donative of land and money and then cut free to do what he wanted with it all. It had taken twenty five years service to win it and Falerius was confident that this emperor would honour his pledge to reward military service. He kissed her tenderly on the lips, told her to get word to him if she needed anything and left for the bath house. Family life was something to fight for, a security, and the army secretly enjoyed it as it often provided new troops for the future. Yet it often came second best to the comradeship of men who had endured deprivations, dangers and war and who had successfully come through it all. That was a bond of strength.

The bath house fire was smoking nicely. Lit and washed down early in the morning the building was doing a good trade with weary soldiers eager to get heat back into stiff joints and muscles that had been so used to carrying weight on one side of the body. These could now be stretched and pummelled back into some kind of use. It was a social draw for everybody except the higher ranking officers who had their own private domestic baths within their houses in the fort. Even so the atmosphere was disciplined yet relaxed with gambling and games mixing side by side. Falerius took off his tunic, sandals and licium and walked into the whitewashed caldarium room where steam gently billowed out from holes in the wall. Like damp smoke it gently swirled and rose high to the vaulted ceiling where it hung until falling back to the tiled floor via droplets of moisture. He took his place on the stone bench and as the mist worked its warm trickery on him he began to notice reddening scars that hadn't been too evident before. It wasn't important. On a battlefield there had been a medical corps but as military hospitals were too far away to be safely reached, many would die of their wounds. The scars were a reminder of fortune and good luck to the living. Falerius felt like living.

The cleansing warmth of the steam, the gentle hubbub of voices and the overheard sexual boasts of the vain mixed with the knowledge that this was a province hopefully at peace, gave him confidence for the future. He thought of his farm somewhere and an end to all the fighting, taking his place proudly in the new evolving rich countryside, a land that he had helped to forge and on which he would be keen to make his mark with all the skills that the army had shown him. He left the hot room, beads of sweat following behind and without ceremony sank into the icy cold of the plunge pool where his muscles tightened again to meet every oncoming challenge. A rubbing down afterwards followed by an application of perfumed oils transformed him into the true citizen. After dressing again and walking out into the shallow warmth of a bright September's day Falerius felt lighter and hungrier for life itself.

Back in his room a bowl of warm pork stew had been arranged with more bread, cheese and sweet biscuits, a little honey and a small jug of watered wine to wash it down. Outside his bedroom wall the horns continued to sound the watches and troops clanked past for their duties. Military life continued unabated. There was a knock at the door.

'Centurion Julianus Falerius Silvanus, excuse my intrusion. Can you spare a little time?' In the doorway stood the figure of a man not far off six feet tall and of a thin but strong appearance. He wore a tunic of coarse wool, dyed a mustard yellow colour, tied knee length with a belt and had a groomed beard with intelligent eyes set upon a kind face.

'Cominius, it's good to see you again. I trust that you are well.' Falerius rose and grasped his friend by the wrist in a friendly handshake. 'I see the journey home has been favourable. Have you also worn your feet out on the roads of Britannia? What can I do for you?'

Cominius knew that he needn't watch his words, for Falerius had a reputation for fairness. He hadn't been the stick wielding centurion of old beating his century like dogs and then dying like a dog himself as mutinies erupted. He had led by example and although despising the cowardly had shown the path to bravery to all. Many of his men were still alive.

'Falerius, I have come to repay my debt of honour to you, an overdue one and I am now in the position to do so. You saved my life, remember?' He recounted the afternoon his surveying team were engaged on setting the line for a new road when they were suddenly attacked by spear wielding barbarians riding nothing more than small ponies. 'We were without an escort and you came quickly to my aid. By covering me with your shield you saved my life but were wounded yourself by the spear thrust.'

'An act any soldier would have done,' commented Falerius, 'I shall no doubt receive my corona aurea in due course,' he quipped.

'That is as may be,' Cominius continued. 'My understanding is that you are due your discharge shortly and I wondered what it was that you were going to do? The land about here isn't particularly fertile and the crops limited. The markets as they are growing are all to the East and there are still hidden riches to be won from the soil. Let me show you . . .' He rolled a vellum map out and smoothed it flat with the palm of his hand. 'This is where we are. Notice the road network that is serving the province and the towns that are growing too. As you appreciate Falerius, my job is to dig the army into where it needs to be, fortlets, roads, public buildings sometimes, that kind of thing. I dig holes and then I look into them for nobody wants a road or a building to slump into the ground because of lack of planning. Permanence is my watchword, to ensure that nothing is ever left to chance. This is where I am able to help you.'

Falerius looked on deeply interested in the map and the spread of the influence the army now had on the island and how the veins of communication were reaching out to places not even he had seen or heard about. 'This is the whole province, Cominius, what do you have in your mind to propose?'

'Well, I remember about ten years ago we were engaged on a civilian project of building new granaries here,' and he pointed at the map, 'on the road from Calleva to Glevum at Durocornovium. The soil was as you saw on the surface, good sandy soil that was easily drained and easily ploughed but it was what was beneath that was of more interest. My surveying officer, an Hispanic, recognised it as being similar earth to what he had seen in Italia for cleaning and improving woollen fleeces. Its texture is firm and the colour a green blue. Scratch it with your finger nails and you will never forget it. It is like wax. We kept our find quiet for we didn't want to rouse the interest of the local tax official or the procurator who may have seized it for the emperor and it was to be our pension.'

'The two of you have kept this quiet? How much is there and what do I know about a quarry? Won't a sudden large hole prove a little obvious?' Falerius was riddled with doubt and lacked the self confidence of a merchant to want to take it any further.

'No Falerius, the clay is disguised amongst reeds and hard grasses. The Celts, who have never taken advantage of it because they never needed to or understood how to, have left the land largely as it was. A simple drainage plan will give you the advantage of taking the mineral out little by little as it lies close to the surface in some places. Furthermore you can disguise the land by having sheep upon it and build yourself a nice little business all in one place. With the roads and ever improving markets, you will have a living for yourself and your son. I can help you acquire it all if you so wish.'

'And your share Cominius. You must want a return yourself?'

'Yes, I shall invest in you to begin with and then I may return one day and lay a claim to it or I may stay here looking for gold in the mountains to the north and west of us. The gold or the clay, Falerius, what would you choose if you were me?'

'The other officer, the Hispanic, where is he?' Falerius had to ask.

'He's dead. I can send a trusted slave out, if you like, to find you a price for the land. No doubt a retiring legionary centurion will carry enough weight to persuade the landowner to sell his waterlogged fields to you. We are all due our stipendiary soon and you must have savings?' Falerius blushed. Bribes he meant from his men to avoid the most irksome of duties. 'Yes there is money,' he replied.

'Good, then I will see to it that a fair price is negotiated and will contact you again shortly. Please keep this quiet. Your son, Falerius, may grow up prosperous and not have to live his life out in the shadow of the camp like yourself. I trust that my debt to you is settled?' He shook him firmly by the wrist and left.

The autumn of that year slipped quietly into winter. The roads were empty save for the usual military patrols and Falerius marked the boredom of static garrison life by attending the festivals that marked the year's end. All being well, if he could maintain himself for another month without falling susceptible to fever or death from lingering wounds then he would collect his donative and be free. Another life beckoned beyond the walls yet he was grateful for the chance to stay although he had to work for it. The new recruits had joined and bolstered the depleted ranks but they needed bringing on in mental and physical strengths – fighting, marching, digging and parading. Falerius too had named his replacement for promotion and he would be sworn in at the beginning of the new year when all renewed their vows of loyalty to the Gods, the Emperor and the army itself. Shortly afterwards Falerius would be discharged.

That day soon arrived and with due courtesy Falerius was summoned to the Principia building.

'Julianus Falerius Silvanus, Centurio of VII cohort Legio Secunda Augusta, in the name of the Emperor Caesar Hadrianus you are hereby discharged with honour from your service and free to return to civilian life.' Sitting behind a sloping writing desk, the tessarius spoke slowly and carefully. In the ante room with them stood the signifier, the cohort's standard bearer and also treasurer.

'Owing to you from your payment of 5,000 denarii a year,' the signifier said, 'there is this amount,' and the tessarius looked over to check, running his finger down a column of figures. 'Owing to the army of the province of Britannia there is this amount!' The figures were for stores and equipment although Falerius had been able to buy most of his more valuable assets, his sword included, himself. 'Then there are your personal savings deposited with the cohort, your deposits and of course the generous discharge payment from our gracious emperor. The final figure is here,' the tessarius concluded. It wasn't an insubstantial figure. 'You may leave the army's property with the stores and may I wish you on behalf of your men, health, and a long life.' He proceeded to hand Falerius a written copy of his military service and politely enquired about the plans that Falerius had.

'You will understand the great difficulty our emperor has had in deciding to abolish gifts of land, Falerius,' he added as if he knew the emperor personally; although Falerius recognised in his voice the necessity of officialdom however tedious. He was simply relaying the imperial message.

As to the land Falerius was undecided. He had risked his life on many occasions but not merely to dispossess an innocent family of their lands. Additionally Cominius had warned him of the fertility of the soil hereabouts and as far as he was concerned plans were already in place to buy his way into a richer life elsewhere. It was simple now – take the money and leave.

The door of the ante room opened out into a small courtyard where others waited to be called in. There was an audible excitement about the place as Falerius politely pushed his way towards the main entrance, his shoulders being slapped by old friends as he passed. Before him stood the imposing granaries with their massive buttressed walls, the swept streets and rows of barrack blocks and workshops all built by human hands and all a vital part in the army's existence whilst it was away fighting. Falerius made himself a vow that his fields were to be orderly, his home clean and his slaves, if he had many, were to be the best that he could afford. His remaining years were to be guarded by order and obedience to it. With this increasing impatience he couldn't wait to take part in the rich vein of provincial life and felt that he had the necessary skills to succeed.

CHAPTER III

MERCURY'S HAND

Cominius was as good as his word. A settlement on the land concealing the clay was agreed without breaking too much into Falerius' savings, and the family owning it more than happy to move on. The Romano British world had suddenly enriched them and in doing so provided them with a choice. They were free and in that freedom chose to move to a relative's estate not too far away and help enlarge it. They would also, as a condition of the purchase, continue to care for it until Falerius had arrived to take up occupancy, not that there was much to care for. They had lived there for generations unmolested by the roman armies moving north and west and when questioned about the white horse carving on the hillside above knew little about it as the old traditions were oral and most of the stories forgotten or no longer required telling. Along with the new masters came a new order and that included their new gods.

The slave, Marcus, had also reported that the old Celt hadn't cared for the military and wasn't too concerned either with the fighting, far away to the north. The living here was good with a certain amount of safety to be found. He and his family could move between the two worlds and absorb new ideas as money dictated. There were new towns growing up, new meeting places, exotic buildings of stone and unavoidably the new taxes to pay for it all. Many still continued to eke out a meagre living surrounded by the rich elite yet little by little they were showing their obedience to it in the form of learning the language, adopting the new dress and trying new technologies and new foods. Why then, the old man had asked Marcus, was somebody interested in land that was cold and wet with slopes that faced north? What value was there in it? Had he found himself a stupid Roman?

A few days later and Falerius, with family, was ready to go.

'Falerius, may you and your family travel safely, watched over by the gods.' Cominius was waiting for them at the edge of the vicus to wish them well and to tie up his part in the deal. The laden cart with Falerius, Julia and Attius in, together with the necessary items for a week on the road, rumbled up and stopped.

'You are going to need Marcus here to guide you but I have given him enough money to travel with so please do not worry. He will help to establish you in your new home and when you are finally settled, the gods permitting, I will take leave to travel and see you.'

'To come and see your share, Cominius, no doubt. Your share of my hard work.' Falerius joked and Julia laughed alongside.

'That is as may be but remember to go about your business slowly. It will need a little time to ripen or else others may prey upon you and it all sickens because of it. This is your son's inheritance Falerius, something for him. Keep him out of the army's reach if you can and make him a rich man!'

That said Falerius and Cominius embraced with Julia and Attius unable to comprehend the bond of friendship from their cart. A debt of honour meant so little to them except that somebody had given them the chance of a permanent home and for that reason alone they would be eternally grateful. Cominius would be welcome at any time.

The impatience of Marcus's horse reminded them to be off. It was early and to make Glevum was their first task before embarking on the onerous climb above the old fortress town and to Corinium and beyond. It seemed to take ages for the cart and horse to become smaller on the straight edges of the road yet Cominius watched them for as long as he could. In his heart he wished that he were going too but a host of money making opportunities still remained locked away in his writing tablets for others to be drawn into. Digging the land was always going to be more profitable that fighting over it.

Progress for Falerius in the cart was slow. The oxen, tiring on the hills and happier on the flat river valley, plodded on. The short days of February held within them sudden squalls of cold sharp rain and often the four of them would crouch beneath the cart for shelter until it blew over. Mercury would require something before giving sanction to this particular venture and Falerius would carefully unwrap the family's small portable stone altar from its cloth and give due reverence in return for safe passage. Nights were spent shivering around a small fire eating preserved meats and pickles, until they came across a mansio and could enjoy a brief night's rest in relative warmth however many fleas they added to the load. A warm meal supplemented by talk other than that of the military reminded Falerius that indeed this was to be his new life. He felt ignorant of current affairs and in that ignorance hid behind his soldierly exterior and bravely looked out. It was going to take time to change.

All their spirits lifted with the climb away from Glevum. The sky felt closer and the mountains of Siluria receded far into the distance. Falerius would often stop the cart and point out to Julia and Attius where they had come from, Marcus pointing the opposite way to where they were heading. Corinium came and went, Durocornovium next, followed by another steep climb to meet the old Celtic track way heading east. They were almost there.

Traffic on the ancient way was sparse. Nobody would ever risk valuable cargo up here either through banditry or breakages. In winter the chalk surface was soft after the rain and the cart slid from rut to rut like a floundering ship amongst white breakers. Progress seemed to slow down considerably. There were no grand gated villa entrances here with slaves to seek help from, no smooth gravelled surfaces to provide grip and the track way appeared little more than a minor blood vessel pumping the vital life goods around the province. In winter it was desolate and so thoroughly abandoned that the roman world appeared to pass it by. The roads hastily chasing the wars to the north and west charged through it without stopping and the bewildered tribesmen left behind had taken a little organising into building a new world. The area was a backwater devoid of anything of value. It certainly wasn't as Falerius had imagined. He wanted company and an orderly way of life with established routine. He thought of the veteran colonies of Isca far behind and wondered at what he had chosen to do.

Marcus had suggested that they drop down into the vale below not only for shelter from the weather but also to help the oxen as the land was flat. It wasn't far to go he kept on reassuring them but Falerius was finding it hard to release his military thinking that high ground was always safety. He still had his sword hidden and wrapped away on the cart but relaxed a little at the prospect of this already being fought over safe land. Even so Glevum, Corinium or even Calleva were far away and what military presence was there going to be hereabouts. What chance of a cavalry patrol passing – little. The oxen plodded on unaware that their toil was close to an end.

'Centurion Falerius, we are here,' Marcus said in a direct manner unaware of his addressing Falerius as Centurion. It had passed Falerius by.

A mud track led to a large yard with an orchard off to one side. Around it were cords of timber with old barns close to dereliction containing the winter fodder. Directly in front was the small house fashioned in a mix of the old and the new. Wattle and daub walls held up a stone tiled roof, but only just, and wooden shutters over the open window frames were ill fitting. Attius was sent to recover some firewood in the small copse behind whilst Falerius helped Julia down from the cart.

'Has good fortune brought us here?' she asked, wrapping the cloak warmly around her yet feeling colder now the motion of travel had stopped. The farmyard felt too close to the hills for her as if the cold northerly winds would fail to climb over them and lie in the valley bottom forever. Would the sun rise over the hills and would it ever be warm?

'Good fortune is here, Julia, although we may not be seeing it. Trust in the gods,' Falerius reassured her.

Marcus went to the door and announced their arrival to the incumbent. The Celt who came out was like his house, half and half. He too wore a thick woollen cloak fastened with a stout roman brooch with woollen leggings to cover his legs. On his feet he wore solid leather boots but his appearance was very much native; his hair long and face unshaven. Marcus drew him cautiously towards the cart. Brief introductions were made and the two men eyed each other with mutual suspicion. Falerius' experience of the native world was through force however much he restrained from using it. The option was always there and often sanctioned by his senior officers. The will of Rome had to be understood. The old farmer saw in Falerius the changing world that was creeping in. His generations had tried to rid the island of the Romans but had to bend their limbs beneath the yoke. They adopted the customs slowly and in their way. There were too few examples of roman life here, and unless bullied into taking their part, it would remain so for the native Celts. Falerius had to be an ambassador and although he couldn't see it, the perfumed Roman oils had only washed over the mud stained Celtic world; they had yet to be fully absorbed beneath the skin.

The old man spluttered a few words of Latin, which Falerius acknowledged. A chest was taken off the cart and the remaining silver deposit handed over. He scratched at the coins with his fingers and then bit them between his teeth misunderstanding the sincerity that the emperors were minting for all and sundry – 'Public Hope, The Best of Emperors and the Peace of the Army.' It was all an irrelevance, for the old man had no idea of an empire. Real power to him lay in the growing local town of Durocornovium where a few of his number had already found influence, yet that influence came with an obligation to spend their money promoting the public good in the shape of new buildings and other public works. The old farmer was wiser than that. He hid his money closer to his heart and, having reassured himself that the coinage was good, departed on his cart.

'Marcus, how long are you planning to stay?' Falerius asked. It was an important question.

'Two days I thought, Falerius. On my way back to Isca I will register your tax holding and mark you down as the landholder in Duro-cornovium. After that I will have to return but all the formalities will have been completed. Are you pleased?' Marcus answered. In the afternoon of an early spring day, in a vale unknown to him and now unburdened by a major part of his wealth Falerius was unsure. Holding Julia by the hand and revolving slowly around, he took measure of his estate. The small puddled fields that were damaged from over-wintering stock stretched away and the orchard looked unpruned and unproductive. Everywhere fences were weak and required mending with thin crops poking their heads out from amongst the weeds. Marcus' help was going to be sorely needed. An officer back in Isca had lent him a book on current farming methods that he may find useful although written with the warmer climate of Gaul in mind. It advocated when to plant, what to plant, how to control diseases and how to rear healthy stock. Falerius had to place great faith in it whilst Ceres quietly looked over his shoulder.

When Attius had returned with sufficient firewood to keep them warm for the day they all retired indoors. The little rectangular building stunk of a cold hammered chalk floor and of wet animal skins and smoke. Without troops to order in and clean the place it was going to take Falerius a while to come to terms with it all. The lack of sanitation, the structure of the building, the total lack of furnishings and the land all required his immediate attention. Furthermore, what of the clay? He needed to be thinking about that as soon as possible in order to see a return on his money. That was going to require slaves and a trip to the market place. There were animals to buy, iron tools and seeds to plant so that they might eat. Attius now a strong keen lad could help with the land whilst Julia could look after the garden and food. Falerius could oversee it all – the veteran, soldier farmer. Sitting down with Marcus that first evening of their arrival he was keen to make a start.

The warming longer days of the unfolding year made life easier and with military precision Falerius dug the first of his ditches finding the clay that Cominius had seen. It was exactly as he had described. Green, cold and soft deeper down with the texture of wax but closer to the surface it was harder and required a sharp twist of the wrists to break apart. Falerius was drawn by it. How was this going to make him rich?

'Father, is it market day soon?' The young Attius enquired looking into the hole. 'Can I buy the sheep and the man to look after them?'

'Yes, son.' Falerius cautiously replied not wanting to promise too much. Marcus had left a while ago and he felt very much now on his own. A slave could be company but only if educated. He knew there to be a market in Corinium, a day's ride away, yet to buy in human flesh was at odds for him. Slaves had often been distributed at the end of a campaign season and he had been more accustomed to selling them for a profit than having to provide for them. However the facts were that he needed help and he could afford one good one at the very least. He climbed out of the earth, grabbed Attius around the waist and marched home with him.

Julia herself was doing well with the garden and the house, although requiring rebuilding, served them adequately basking in the warm sunlight falling from the sky. Everything looked better. Apple, pear and plum blossom had fallen in the orchard and in the not unsubstantial vegetable garden; artichokes, asparagus and cucumbers were supplying the larder. With Falerius managing to buy a few pigs from a neighbour the family were learning to survive outside the army. Then with the acquisition of a slave renamed Longinus by Falerius, work at last progressed on the land itself.

Attius' sheep were introduced to the fields first concealing the clay, along with a few goats for eating. These were the fields where strange morning mists rose as a precursor to fine days. Longinus, the sheep man as Attius called him, cared for them along with everything else that required caring for. Falerius had chosen well for although not renowned for their intellect, Longinus the Celt was proving a reliable farmhand.

The land obviously required draining as in places the water still lay after a heavy shower and Longinus was instructed to pen off a corner and put all the animals there to eat it down. When they had, this was to be Falerius' first go at digging the clay out but first the ditches had to be marked in order to make it appear that this was their sole objective in owning the land – its drainage and subsequent improvement. Falerius sought out his slave in order to give him the detailed instructions for the following day.

'Longinus, tomorrow we will begin to dig a little soil out. I want to have the clay that is near the surface as it will have been warmed by the sun and is drier. It will be easier to crush into a powder. Also I need you to shear two of the flock and we will try out the powder on those.' His instructions were precise and the following morning the iron tipped wooden spade bit into the soil, Falerius eagerly watching as Longinus turned the sandy topsoil out. 'Avoid the sand,' Falerius barked, intent on the richer veins of clay whilst also aware that the deeper Longinus went the more likelihood there was of water bleeding into the hole from the surrounding earth. 'Let's try what you have found there. Bring two buckets of clay back to the house, I will prepare the vats and Attius can go for the water.' Back at the house the boy was given his instructions. He was to go the spring and fetch enough water for the fleece to be washed in and not to be too long about it. Going there on his own was a great trust for the water had always risen in silent bubbles from the soft white earth and Attius didn't ever want to offend the spirits residing there and cause them to leave and the spring dry up. His father had been too busy to dig a well for the house and the Celts hadn't bothered either so this was their only source. He took great care in filling the buckets and returned to the house where his father was waiting.

'Good boy, now pour it in the tub,' Falerius instructed. 'Fetch the pot full of piss and be careful not to spill any as there isn't enough in all of us to fill it back up again,' Falerius joked, 'especially you. When Longinus returns we will see what we can do with this,' and he held up a fresh bundle of oily sheep skin still sticky with grease. Attius looked at him and asked 'Will this make us rich Father? Can I have a pony and a spear and go hunting for you? Longinus says that there are many fat pigs around us!' The slave wasn't too late in arriving back and his welcome was a swift kick up the backside from his master. 'Those fat pigs around us feed us as well as provide a meal themselves,' he cautioned. Longinus understood the obvious reference and he was to curb his tongue when in Attius' company.

'Longinus, crush the clay into a powder and then add it to the tub. Attius, the piss pot please.' Falerius mixed the two ingredients together to form a grey slippery liquid. 'Sandals off, Longinus, and then I want you to step into the tub. If nothing else it will clean your feet!' Falerius watched as Longinus did as he was told. Warmer water may have helped the mix but that was out of the question for they didn't have that amount of timber on the farm and if they had who would cut and carry it all? The expense would be too great. However he had to try this way first and after a short while the trampled fleece was drawn from the tub, wrung free of its wet load of slippery clay and rinsed clean in fresh water before being allowed to dry out in the sun. After a while an eager Falerius keenly compared the two. The quality was obvious to him. The unwashed fleece smelt of oils but was favoured for being rough, waterproof and warm even when wet. The washed fleece was smoother and felt like it could be worked into a better, more expensive cloth. Falerius realised this and had a marketable product that he could take to town and sell. He was extremely excited at the prospect although there was a lot to do beforehand. The organising was to be his task – digging enough clay out for their needs without attracting attention, buying enough sheep to give the raw material and taking the product to market. He had to swear Longinus to secrecy about their find and told him to keep his mouth shut if seeing slaves working in the neighbouring fields. They were drainage ditches that he was digging, nothing else.

Longinus was put to shearing the remaining flock and that was a hard task for any old hand as the iron clippers required constant sharpening. However with Longinus' skills the valuable cargo was hidden away, water supplies brought to the house and stored in a large stone tank and enough clay dug out to clean the fleeces in the barn and no more. All that was missing was the piss. Falerius wanted to stop using it altogether and experimented without it but it was essential and a mixture of clay and water wasn't proving entirely satisfactory. Furthermore, the more sheep he bought the more piss he would require to treat the oily fleeces. All of them would have to carry a pot with them when in the fields and discharge their load into the latrine at night. When there was sufficient collected, then they could prepare another load for market and so on. It wasn't satisfactory and Falerius knew that the business had to grow. He could try and buy piss from the town and bring it home again but that would be difficult given the nature of the tracks once off the major roads. One breakage and he would be losing money. With the market day close at hand there was going to be competition for wool sales especially from the military buyers looking for new stocks from which to produce tunics and cloaks. They weren't going to worry about the oils in the fleece as all soldiers stunk on campaign as Falerius knew and even in the worst of weathers they were good at keeping the wearer warm and dry. It was to the fashionable villa owners that Falerius had an eye. He had seen them in his army days strutting about in their fine tunics and cloaks sourced from the best of suppliers. He had heard talk from the fine dining tables of fabulous costume and food. The season for wool and status was going to be short and Falerius had but a little time to prepare.

As the evening mists once again drew their palms over the damp land and as Falerius watched Julia carefully pick her way to the latrine before dark he trusted that winged Mercury would be kind and agree to his venture. He would offer a sacrifice and ask. If Attius was to have his pony and his spears then there was going to be a lot for his father to learn.

CHAPTER IV

SILVER

The journey to market in Corinium seemed to Falerius a retrograde step into his military roots and backwards towards Isca. It had been half a year and more since his leaving and in that time he had bought land, moved his family and also established a small business. He was in a confident mood then as he watched Longinus hitch up the light wagon to the mule as speed not strength was to be the order of the day. The road that he was getting to know so well was becoming a chore to travel and in the back of his mind future journeys to market would be undertaken by Attius or Longinus. Falerius would relax at home.

'Longinus, be careful with the skins. Keep them flat and protect them from the dust. I want buyers to see them at their best if we are to attract a good price,' Falerius barked. 'I'll find Attius and then be ready to go!'

Attius emerged from the darkness of the house at his father's calling. Julia followed and stood in the doorway watching the three of them getting ready.

'I hope to be back tomorrow.' Falerius spoke quietly as if not wishing to be overheard or anybody have knowledge of his whereabouts. 'If you are worried by anything then close and bolt the door. If needs be then come and meet me on the Corinium road. I'd leave Longinus but we need him to see to the animal. You know where I hide the sword so keep yourself safe.' He kissed her tenderly with promises of a bag full of money and turned to Attius. 'Come on, jump up, and let's go.'

The cart once again rumbled off to meet the main road north at Durocornovium, the skins bouncing about quietly in the back. Julia returned their waves and went back into the house. As they travelled past the half eaten, damp, half drained fields Falerius began to dream of profits to come. From his vantage point he imagined a thousand sheep, an opulent house and a lifestyle to match. He was to be a man of standing, a military advisor that people could turn to in times of trouble. How deep to dig their ditches? How best to build a wall and how to build a road that would last without constant repair? He would buy a toga and take an interest in the peace that he had helped to forge. First though, he would like to bark out orders and clear the road of unnecessary stragglers who were impeding his progress and his plans, for the way to market was now filling up from all directions. By the third hour of the day they had made good progress and by the fifth they had arrived.

Market day traffic had slowed their pace to a crawl as they headed towards the largest obvious building to be seen – the Forum. At little more than walking pace, Attius could see what he had missed when they had made the journey to their new home through this same town. The half timbered houses were taller than his and had more shuttered windows. The streets were pleasant and not rutted although a little dusty with all the traffic of the day. Dotted amongst the tenement blocks were small fields like theirs containing animals with adjacent farmhouses surround-ed by high walls. There were far more people than Attius was used to seeing, other than soldiers, some of them wearing the toga although most in tunics; and the noise they were making! In the west, he could just make out the low grassy relief of the amphitheatre where his father would not take him. That had disappointed Attius as his mother had always told him how the brave gladiator sweat was to be saved for adoring women to buy. Attius made a pact to himself to be brave if that time ever came.

Past workshops the cart was swept up in the mêlée of a crowd wanting to buy and sell. Attius' father was pushed along on a tide of expectation, sailing along in the empire-wide trading winds. Spices, pottery and wine from far off were instant attractions to be having at home. Longinus eventually pulled the cart to a stop. At a convenient place in the street, he was told to remain there whilst Falerius and his son took a few of the fleeces into the broad, flat square of the Forum. There Falerius set a blan-ket on the ground and lay his product out for all to see. He wasn't entirely sure what to do next.

'Father, why don't you shout that you have something to sell?' Attius asked inquisitively.

'The right man will see that we have something here worthwhile to buy,' Falerius reassured him. 'We need to be patient and Mercury will guide us.'

'I'm hungry and thirsty. Can I look around?'

Falerius relented so as not to have any potential business transaction spoilt by his son and gave him a few bronze coins. After that, he was told to report to Longinus and stay there.

People came and people went; the apparently wealthy and otherwise. Some pointed and the slaves carried away what they had pointed at. There were stall holders preparing food whilst blazingly red samian vessels stood out from amongst the orange coppersmiths' wares and silver. The smell of incense carried from shrines wafted amongst the shoppers as if the gods were there in person shopping with them. The hours after midday came and went without an enquiry although some had commented on how fine the wool was to the touch. They personally though didn't have the means to work it into a garment and it would take a factory owner to realise its potential. Falerius was sure that the army trade was going on outside the market place where sheep and cattle had been penned in. With the numbers of sheep hereabouts who was going to pay attention to his few skins and who would want them for themselves? Furthermore as part of any army deal they would insist upon delivery to one of their warehouses which could be anywhere. Falerius tried hard not to feel dejected at having a product that he could not sell in the largest of markets around. He would simply have to take it home again and try another day, not particularly relishing the journey.

'That is fine wool to my eye. How much do you have to sell?' The voice spoke as the fingers caressed the silky fibres between them. 'Are you local?'

'Yes. No.' Falerius spluttered. 'We've come to market today. My son is about here somewhere and my slave is with the cart. Are you looking to buy?'

'There is every possibility,' the stranger continued. 'This is indeed the best quality wool that I have seen in this town for a while. What is your secret?' He leant forward.

'Good piss.' Falerius offered as a reason and the two men laughed. Falerius clutched at his own groin in a mocking gesture.

'Let me introduce myself,' the stranger spoke. 'My name is Cornix and I am the estate bailiff for my master Gaius Helvius Bonus, magistrate of Corinium. He has a mind to invest in local producers so that they may share in his wealth. He may be interested in sending these on to Londinium where they could be finished off and sold in Gaul and Germania. There may be a good price for you if I am allowed to go and speak with him. Are you here long?'

Falerius naively misunderstood the question. 'I will have to return home tomorrow. Can you get there and back in that time?'

'My master has a town house here. Currently he is with friends but I can be back within the hour with his answer and . . .' Cornix tapped his money belt, 'a little profit for you as well. Accept my apologies. You are?'

'My name is Julianus Falerius Silvanus, ex-centurion of the Second Augustan Legion.'

'Then you are a man of true bravery. I could see it all along,' Cornix boasted.

Falerius was elated at the prospect of a sale although his potential buyer had soon melted away into the thinning crowds without having handed over anything. He could do with the money to buy the evening meal but in order to eke out what he had left, Falerius decided to camp outside the town that night, as the weather was good, and to set off for home first thing in the morning. When Attius returned he uninterruptedly told his father of all the wonders that he had seen, although he swore that he hadn't been anywhere near the amphitheatre. He had instead seen doctors, priests, the baths and all kinds of foods that he didn't recognise as growing in his mother's garden. There were too many people though for his comfort and one of them was talking to Longinus.

'He may know somebody,' Falerius answered.

'No father, he was better dressed,' Attius offered as an observation. 'He had a clean tunic and a broad brimmed hat.'

'It sounds like the man that approached me about the wool. I'll talk to Longinus about it later. First help me roll up these skins and then show me where the food is!'

The pair of them returned the goods to the cart and Longinus was instructed to stay there with them. Upon their return, he could go for his own supper. Falerius and his son then set off for the short walk to the cross-roads in the centre of Corinium where the best shops appeared to be. The food stall itself consisted of a low building with a long wooden bench at the front from which food was served. Behind it was the work area where the meals were prepared or where they quietly bubbled away. A portly man stood guard behind the counter and Attius watched with interest as he took his father's order and placed it on the iron grid above the fire. Smoke from the offering rose into the warm evening sky and then curled in upon itself before disappearing into many dark mysterious atoms.

'He's offering our food to the gods, father!' cried Attius.

'Only one part of it, son. There is still enough left for me.' Shortly afterwards the sausages and a bowl of vegetable stew was placed on the counter along with a piece of broken bread to mop up the liquid. Attius grimaced at the strange tastes but was reassured that they were only spices intended to improve the taste and not hide the quality. A dish of warm dates cooked in honey improved his appetite and he ate it all.

'Not eating the horseflesh sausages, Falerius? I can recommend better,' Cornix remarked as he peered over Falerius' shoulder. 'Your slave showed me where to find you.'

'And I can recommend that you eat somewhere else,' the shopkeeper grimaced holding up a knife with a sausage still attached. 'You'll ruin my trade,' he moaned.

'Have you still an appetite for business, Falerius? We need to talk.' By lowering his head, Cornix dropped into a whisper. 'Follow me.' The two of them moved away into the middle of the street where the day's traffic had ceased. 'May the gods rot your stomachs!' the stall keeper's curse following them. 'The fool's drawing attention to himself and his rotten food. He'd be better served by silence,' Cornix observed. He lowered his head and again began to whisper. 'My master is interested in your wool. He has friends that can take it back to Londinium as a return load when bringing produce here to market. They bring in wine amphora and dates and return with wool, usually the coarse type that is then made into cloaks to sell on the markets in Gaul, sometimes Rome itself. I took a piece with me for him to try and it soaked up the red wine in his beaker admirably. He feels therefore that it will take a good dye and be true in colour. How much have you to sell. Is this it?' Falerius was excited at the uninvited trial and Cornix had offered information that he hadn't asked for. Suddenly he felt businesslike and rapidly offered the one hundred fleeces that he had brought with him. 'That's not many, Falerius. New markets are already opening in Calleva and Verulamium as well as Londinium itself. We will require more and to achieve this, my master will want to invest his money in you so that you can share in his future wealth.' Cornix shook a leather pouch and it rattled to the sound of silver. The deal was before him. Falerius was to hand over the wool and Cornix the silver. However, what about Cominius and his say? He wasn't there to speak and Falerius could only guess at his answer.

'We propose meeting with you and I am here to offer a dinner invitation to my master's house just outside Durocornovium on the road to Leucomagus in say, ten day's time. Do you know the house? He wishes that we could discuss business in a more relaxed atmosphere and with other clients of his. May I take your answer?' Cornix was immediately to the point.

'An answer to the meal invitation or the investment opportunity?' queried Falerius, not wishing to show his naivety in matters of business.

I'll need a little time to think and I will send Longinus over with a reply. Ten days ought to be sufficient for me to make a decision,' he confidently concluded. 'I would like to sell this load of wool today though.'

'By way of my master's generosity, what price for one hundred fleeces?'

The two men settled on the price. Falerius was unsure as to its real worth but was happy at being able to return home with something. As part of the deal, he was instructed to drop the load off at a small warehouse in Durocornovium that belonged to the magistrate. Ten days forth he was to dine with his potential patron and investor. The day had ended too quickly for Falerius and having to think for himself had proved challenging. He no longer had a sword for which he could use to fend off the business proposals put forward and he simply couldn't turn and run away from an offer, any offer. He had to go with his instincts. At Longinus' return from supper he was more than happy to be feeling the motion of the cart beneath him as it departed the town and made for the serenity of the roadside where he could find some peace of mind and think. Attius from his perch in the rear watched as the torch lights of Corinium grew fainter and the hubbub, less. Alongside the road weary travellers were already making provision for a night's rest to save themselves the expense of a room in the mansio. Silently the constellations moved in their transit above and the gods looked down.

'Father, we didn't buy any piss or a pony!'

Julia waited at the end of their fields for the sight of a distant wagon. Two hours had passed by and the clouds slowly made their way towards the west at little more than walking pace. A slight breeze parted the stalks of grass around where she was standing alone, the only other signs of life being labourers toiling away in the heat haze beyond. Last night had been too quiet for her without the once regular watches being called from the fort or the warmth of another human being. She had slept but an hour at the most worrying about Attius. His father could have lost his life many times in the past in remote and lonely spots that few would ever visit again but their son was all she had. This wasn't her homeland and these weren't her people either, yet she accepted that they had to eventually settle somewhere and, in the warm breeze that flowed over her now, she acknowledged that this was for the time being a good home. Fate was firmly with them.

A shout broke into her tired thoughts.

'Mother, we are rich! We are rich! See what I have!' Attius sped towards her having dismounted early from the cart. 'Look!' He thrust his arm out and carefully unrolled his hand to reveal a solitary silver coin. 'Look Mother, we have been given fine money but Father said not to drop it as we will not find another one. Come and look at my pony!' Julia knew that at his age there would be little doubt that she could have survived the night alone and that no harm would have come her way: Treasure was always more appealing than the boredom of potential danger. Falerius knew different and as the cart stopped he handed the reins to Longinus and jumped down to the warm earth below.

'We have done well, as reports will have told.' Falerius pointed at the messenger now trying to untie the pony from the rear of the cart. 'It's his reward.'

'And the other?' Julia said pointing at the second, not so grand pony tied up alongside it. 'Has the money all gone! If so, you'd better keep this safe somewhere,' returning the single silver coin of Attius. 'They came as a pair,' Falerius tried to offer in explanation 'and I thought that Longinus could be put to work teaching him to ride.'

'Why are you late? I haven't seen anybody to talk to,' Julia complained, quizzing him about the hour of his return.

'I've taken the wool to my new patron's warehouse in Durocornovium where he also owns a house on the outskirts of the town. I have been offered a dinner invitation with him in ten day's time to discuss supplying him and his friends in Londinium with our produce. It has happened all so quickly but it is what I have wanted. Come to the house and I will tell you how it all happened. We are blessed by the gods' Falerius blurted out. The door closed behind Attius' parents but he wasn't interested and instead followed Longinus to the barn where he was busy unhitching the mule. That done the animal was led to its paddock and released.

'Can we go riding now, Longinus? My father has gone inside and will be resting for the day.' Longinus himself wasn't too sure of that and explained that he had jobs to be doing. There was more clay to be put out to dry as it made it easier to crush into a powder: then there were the sheep to check and move onto new pastures if necessary and when that was done, there were the ditches to be cleared out if they had filled back in again. The water had to be draining away into the nearby stream to make the clay accessible. When all that was done then, yes, he might have a little time left to give riding lessons. Attius, though, had to play his part.

'Go off into the small wood but stay close to the farm and find yourself a spear,' Longinus told the eager boy. 'A good one that will fly straight and true towards your enemies and when you have chosen it we will return and cut it down. Can you do that?' He then disappeared in order to make it harder for Attius to select a weapon too readily and return to tell him so. The journey back from market had been one full of talk for the future. More sheep meant more clay; more dinners and more silver. Unfortunately for Longinus it also meant more work. Inside the house Falerius was full of boast. 'Cominius has given us new hope with this farm. I've repaid his trust with the best price in the market and he is going to be pleased with the result.'

'Who is this Gaius Helvius Bonus? What do you know of him and can you trust him? Why are you going to dine with him? Are you planning on telling Cominius about this?' A frustrated Julia was full to the brim of business talk. 'Are you going to cloak this island in wool?' she added sarcastically.

'I have offered him nothing, Julia. Except for him to buy from me and I will need to make some friends if I am going to succeed. You know that. We will dine with him and make a decision afterwards. He is an influential man. In the meantime there is a little money left and perhaps, I could buy you something that you would like.' Falerius, seduced by the warm day's sunshine and the constant thought of power imagined two bodies lying on the bed covered in sweat then quietly slipping away into relaxed sleep. He took Julia by the hand and led her on. The land too went to sleep. Longinus moved silently amongst the sheep and Attius carefully examined all the spears in the wood. In the neighbouring fields the scythes silently and effortlessly cut the golden corn.

'Longinus, I've found a spear. When you have eaten your food can we go and cut it?' Attius watched him eagerly for he knew that the answer would not be 'No.' 'Fetch the pony instead Attius, we'll start with that,' Longinus wearily conceded, and with the return of the animal Longinus set about the first lesson in what to look out for. He then questioned the boy thoroughly. 'What do we do first, Attius. What about the eye of the beast and his ears? Look at how he stands. What about his back? Is he lame to you and is his coat clean and shiny? Is he as strong as he looks? Do you think that he will do for you?'

'I like him!' was Attius' simple reply, 'and I think he likes me. I'm going to name him Roma like I have the horse on the hillside. Can we ride up there today?'

'No. There aren't enough hours left now but maybe tomorrow if your father agrees. Put the pony back and let's see about cutting your spear.'

Attius wanted his father to be present at such an important military moment but was nearly scolded for his impatience as he burst into the house unannounced. His father would be there but in his own time, and Attius would have to be patient and wait a short while, for Falerius had nearly finished what he was doing. An hour later towards dark he emerged in a tunic loosely tied about his middle and wearing a pair of simple sandals. He stretched and yawned as he walked towards the wood. Attius wasn't going to question his time keeping and didn't understand the knowing smile that he gave Longinus as he approached.

'Which one is it, soldier? Which one have you chosen to defend us with?' Falerius enquired, knife at the ready.

The blade easily cut away at the straight hazel shaft and it fell to the ground. 'Longinus will clean it up for you. Now we must thank Silvanus for his gift of wood!' Falerius spoke offering a verbal gift with promises of better to come for the deity having left the house unprepared. We will return with a gift tomorrow.'

For the next seven days Longinus became teacher to the young boy's riding ambition. Roma was a new friend to Attius and apart from the slave there wasn't really anybody else to talk to or play with. Hours at the day's end were often spent in training both pony and rider to understand each other and to learn to work together. Attius was put to saddling the pony, grooming it, checking its health and riding endless circles in the tiny paddock reserved for it. For the young boy this soon became boring and he constantly asked to be taken further afield. 'Can we ride up to see the strange horse yet?' He enquired of Longinus. 'That's a morning's work, Attius. I will need your father's permission first.' His answer was carefully put as Longinus didn't want to undermine Falerius. He was the soldier cum rider but what did it matter for the master was becoming obsessed with figures. Every day Falerius would follow Julia about pointing out how they could improve their lives if only he could supply product in large enough numbers. Permission therefore was easily given for Longinus to leave the farm. 'Be careful with the boy. He can wear the best out!' Falerius warned the slave.

The following day Longinus saddled the pony for Attius and placed a good rug over the back of the older animal for himself. He then legged the boy up into his saddle and effortlessly leapt onto his own beast. 'Can you show me that when we return?' Attius said from the security of his mount. 'How you jump onto the pony's back.' More of Attius' seemingly endless demands yet today Longinus didn't mind for he was escaping the endless toil of digging out the clay, and relaxing instead. He had taken the opportunity of approaching Julia for a small meal to take with them and she had supplied the two of them with something from the kitchen. There was bread, cheese and fruit from her own garden all concealed in a leather bag for Longinus to carry over his shoulder.

'We can be the horse riders of Rome itself, Longinus; marking and patrolling the boundaries and then reporting back. The farm is our fortress,' cried out a buoyant Attius as his pony carried him forward. He pushed Roma into a trot and clutched tightly at the spear held in his right hand. The pony worked hard for him as it struggled at getting a firm grip on the slope leading towards the hills. Where it began to level out Longinus had the need to remind him not to race off. 'Try to canter as we have practiced, Attius. Sit tight.' For every one stride that he took, Longinus was taking two so by moving to the front he could control the speed at which Attius followed. The young boy cried out with the freedom of the hills about him and of the exhilaration and speed that Roma was providing. With the soft turf beneath their feet and no ditches to impede them the pair rapidly made for the ramparts of the old fort lying silently empty.

'Attius, the chalk horse is this way!'

'No slave,' Attius replied. 'We must attack the camp first and then seize the horse for ourselves!' Longinus understood all too well what the young man had said. All throughout his brief life he had been fed tales of conquest from his father and now at last he was free to relive them. Longinus too was no longer the Celt, the opposition but in the eyes of Attius he was there to help the Romans, not to fight them. Only in the mind of the slave was rebellion talked of.

Having sped around the inside of the fort and made Longinus guard one of the entrances whilst he attacked, Attius began to tire. They dismounted and sat, backs to the warm sun and looked out over the vale below. The odd house could be seen along with short pieces of farm track leading nowhere in particular. In the far distance the more important main road was visible cutting through the countryside as if paying little heed to boundary or obstacle on its way. The small town of Duro-cornovium was barely seen as a collection of white reflective shapes whilst the larger settlement of Corinium was little more than a smoke haze rising into the rich blue sky from its golden countryside around. To the east and west and further behind them, ran the hills that they were sitting upon, punctuated occasionally by the sharp relief of other abandoned hillforts jutting out towards the sky. To the south the land levelled out until it met with another ridge carrying the road to Calleva. Here the soil was light and punctuated by many sharp flints that required careful crossing on horseback. Where the small fields ended, a thick layer of grass took over and the scent was a delight to intoxicate anyone. 'What better place than this was there for the gods to live,' thought Attius. He would endeavour to ride over it most days and guard and defend it the best he could. Longinus could help too but under the command of Attius. That would leave his father free to farm below and produce the wool to sell. Attius could be the eyes over which the far horizons, obscured in the valley below, could now be seen.

'Eat up, Attius. We have to return.' Longinus suddenly brought the dreaming to an end but as they slowly made their way back down the slope the boy was elated at having been up to touch the sky. They entered the farmyard and Attius had one more request of Longinus – could he teach him to mount the pony like he had seen him do in the morning. 'If I'm out riding without you and I need to get off then who is there that is going to help me up again?' He intelligently asked. The request was honest and with both ponies being tired from their work Longinus was confident that they would not mind a little more. He asked Attius to tie both animals to a post and in walking back a few steps and then suddenly turning and running, Longinus placed his hands flat on the animal's rear and vaulted onto its back. 'Have a go, Attius, but first try a practice jump and vault over my back.' Longinus crouched down low and as Attius confidently sailed over he encouraged him with 'Well done!! One more go.'

Roma, now unburdened by his saddle twitched at the post as his friend was led out of harm's way and returned to its paddock. It cried out for company and pulled back against the post. Longinus seeing this smacked it hard and rebuked it fiercely for its stupidity. 'Silence!' he shouted.

Attius unaware of the potential for harm walked back to his mark a few paces behind the animal's rear. Roma had done his work for the day and wasn't keen for more. He called out for the unseen pony and it called back raising Longinus' frustration. There was to be this one practice and that was all he agreed to himself. The coat of the pony was a crust of drying sweat and he needed to relax by rolling in the dust. 'Attius now!' he called and the boy ran forward.

'Jump!'

Attius' thin arms couldn't carry the weight of his body and he slid from the animal's shiny backside landing at its side and behind. The pony in the field cried out and again Roma responded by pulling back on the post. Attius, kneeling on the floor scolded Longinus for his rough treatment of his animal. 'You've upset him,' he said slowly getting up. Longinus, tired like they all were, was fed up with the regular insults and beat the pony about its neck for its troubles. It recoiled from this assault and then spent its last energy in a wild kick behind, a kick that caught Attius in the side of his head. The boy fell to the ground clutching the wound and screaming. His parents emerged from the house to witness Longinus frantically rubbing the boy's head. 'Quick, cold water,' he urged.

Julia ran for the water whilst Falerius, no stranger himself to wounds on the battlefield, checked his son over. There was little blood, the boy was conscious and the skull where Roma had kicked him hadn't caved in or felt soft. 'Let's lie you down,' he said carefully picking Attius up in his arms and taking him indoors. Longinus, the Celt, the outsider was left to clear the mess away with the door to the house being firmly shut in his face. Inside Attius was placed on a bed and made comfortable. He could talk and see but his head ached. Falerius would send Longinus to bring a doctor from Durocornovium but until he arrived, Attius was to rest. Julia would sit with him, ensuring occasionally that he could wake from a sleep. To do this Attius had to be gently shaken across the shoulders and he must not be allowed to slip into a deep sleep, not until help had arrived.

The sun had now at last worn itself out and the warmth of day replaced by the deathly chill of night. Across the vale the silent chalk horse looked out whilst far below in the dark a plodding and weary Roma carried Longinus towards Durocornovium.

CHAPTER V

ON THE TABLE

The morning light shone on Attius' face illuminating the pain clearly.

'Mother, I am going to be sick. Can you help me? I feel too weak to stand,' he said.

Julia raised his back up against the cool of the plaster wall and held a cloth in cupped hands beneath his chin. He retched slightly and then with careful fingers poked at the slightly raised flesh on his skull. Pulling his fingers away he looked for blood but there wasn't any. 'My head aches. It's Longinus' fault for hitting my pony.' Julia listened silently for the truth hadn't come out yet. 'Why did Longinus hit Roma? What were you both doing?'

'We were practicing tricks,' Attius offered as an excuse and not wishing to see his father beat the slave because of him.

'Your father is waiting for Longinus to return with a doctor. He has seen many wounds on the battlefield and whilst he would wish that it wasn't his own son, with the blessing of the gods you are more fortunate than others. If Longinus is quick then I don't think that your father will beat him for his stupidity. However if he takes any longer than he has done already then . . .' Julia didn't know what then. 'Come, rest,' she said.

'Which wrong road could that slave have taken?' Falerius exploded in a foul mood as he entered the room. 'The army would have . . .'

'Silence, you're not in the army now,' Julia reminded him, unsure of the wisdom of her remark. 'Our son is awake and talking. That is fine for now. Have patience.'

Falerius knew that time was the best of doctors and thankfully because of the wool sales and his impending meeting with Helvius Brutus they had that time to give. The daylight hours were becoming shorter and those of the night longer. Winter would not be far away. 'Has he spoken of the accident?' Falerius quizzed her. 'Yes,' she answered.

Longinus knocked at the door and was immediately summoned in. He apologised and then explained that he had been all throughout the town asking about a doctor but had been turned away at every house due to the lateness of the hour. 'No slave would grant me access, not at that time of day,' he whimpered. 'The last person that I could think of approaching was the magistrate himself and although not at home his bailiff, Cornix, told me that there wasn't a doctor to be found here and that I would have to travel on to Calleva or Corinium. If Attius' condition was to worsen then Cornix would do his best to help. You only have to ask.'

'You have been to the magistrate's house without permission?' Falerius asked incredulously. 'On whose orders?'

'My own,' he said. Longinus was aware that the truth regarding the boy's injury was out and he was keen to avoid repercussions with a clumsy attempt at repairing the damage.

'And the house itself? Were you admitted?' Falerius went on.

'No, Master. Somebody heard my calling and came to the door in the wall.'

'It is fortunate that the magistrate wasn't at home,' Falerius continued trying hard not to give away his curiosity as to the wealth of his potential patron. 'The house is to the south of Durocornovium and off the road to Venta Belgarum, yes?'

'Yes,' Longinus obediently answered.

'Is it suitably grand?'

'I couldn't see. It was last night and in the dark. It had guardian walls and a stout door. The home of a private person I would say.'

'Good.' Falerius instantly seemed to snap out of his mood. 'Attius it appears isn't going to die and tomorrow, Longinus, you are to return to the home of Helvius Bonus and deliver my dinner acceptance along with the news of my son. You child, are to rest with no exertions and Longinus will do your work as well as his own. Is that understood?' Attius instantly felt better although once again sleep was calling him away. 'I've never slept so much Father, except maybe after we returned from the long journey south. The bed is warm and I am so tired!' He curled up into a ball and was very soon peacefully closing his eyes.

The next few days allowed Attius more rest. He reported the sick feeling subsiding and felt strong enough to stand up out of bed. Falerius knew this to be important and got the boy to move about. 'Can you walk about a little? Can you see us clearly?' The answers to both questions were pleasingly 'Yes.'

'Good. As you know, your mother is to accompany me to an important dinner party. Longinus will be responsible for you and if all goes well then I shall have the funds to have you seen by a doctor. Pray to the gods for their favour in this matter.'

The day of the dinner party had arrived. Longinus was to groom the horse and clean the cart. Next he was to lay out clean clothes for Falerius and Julia to wear. Falerius was off inspecting his stock before returning and casting an eye over the accounts. After all that was the real reason for the invitation. Pleasure and business combined. As a farmer now, Falerius hadn't been slow to notice the shortening grass or the chill in the wind. He had to secure a deal that would put food in their cupboards over winter and provide a market for his goods next spring and hopefully for many seasons after that. The pressure was evident on his face. He had lived with it and learnt to deal with it but a different kind of pressure; the pressure of war where a man could lash out with a sword and take a life before somebody took yours. Then there was all the waiting for something to happen. There was the training that forbade running away and the rewards that could be won by standing your ground and fighting back. All men shouted at the tops of their voices and nobody thought anything of it or deemed it socially barbaric. Whatever it was that helped a man survive the trials of war proved useless outside of it. Falerius was nervous. Disease could take his stock at any moment and his land lost in debt and, although Cominius had a stake in the farm, he was nowhere to be seen. At this moment it appeared that a friend, any friend was better than nothing. The battle to win his share wasn't going to be easy or comfortable yet Falerius wanted this meeting to go ahead and what was more – he looked forward to something better to eat. Maybe that could settle his nerves?

As directed he and Julia arrived safely at the villa of Gaius Helvius Bonus mid afternoon. A slave met them and took the horse and cart to the stables. Another led them through the large wooden door in the wall where Longinus had been met and into the garden. The scent of roses and lavender bathed them in an invisible haze of soft purity that both delighted and lifted the senses, whilst before them a bright pool of water reflected the cornflower blue of the sky from its limestone bowl. A simple hedge of box and laurel marked out the central square around which fluted columns rose to hold the low orange tiled roof of the villa itself. Two or three simply pruned fruit trees of cherry and pear slightly concealed the occasional statue in the background whilst the warmth of the late autumn sun played off the honey coloured limestone building. There was a mystery of colour, texture and scent that Julia felt was missing from her life.

'Falerius, is this for us?' She squeezed his hand in an affirmation for all the business transactions that he was going to make that afternoon. The magistrate's house had a fussy, disarming charm about it that Falerius however struggled to grasp.

'Julianus Falerius Silvanus, welcome! May I introduce myself? I am Gaius Helvius Bonus, magistrate of both Corinium and Durocornovium and large land holder in this area, farmed in my absence by my bailiff Cornix, whom I believe you have met.' Cornix standing slightly behind him lowered his head at the introduction. 'You must be Julia. How is your son?' the magistrate continued offering a fine soft hand for her to touch. It felt oily and smooth and its large puffy fingers were adorned by golden rings. Helvius was a man of medium build and as comfortable in a toga as Falerius used to be in armour. He paid a kind compliment to their dress and asked Falerius if he wished to bathe before eating.

'I have had the slaves working hard to warm the water for my guests.

Shall we not undo their work, Falerius? Come!' He led him on to the side of the main villa entrance and through another door to the side of the house where a small stone building stood issuing smoke from its boiler. The building was already echoing to the sounds of occupancy. A slave came and went with wine. 'My wife will be trying the patience of Julia with talk of the town. We can relax and get to know one another Falerius. What kind of man are you? One I can do business with I hope.' He put an arm around his shoulder and walked on.

Falerius felt uneasy. He had been expecting to eat from the best table around but had few defences against the seemingly endless charm being bestowed upon him. Furthermore they had only just arrived. It was going to be a long and difficult afternoon. Helvius continued with the history of this house. 'The baths are new, Falerius but comfortably small. It means that I can escape myself from the endless round of having to secure dinner invitations from those wealthier than myself.' He looked to Falerius for an acknowledgement of that social fact. Instead Falerius felt insulted but couldn't say so. They were his guests. It was his invitation. What was it going to buy?

Outside the walls traffic struggled to get up the long slight incline of the road as it made its way southwards. Falerius could hear the shouts of the wagon drivers as they exhorted their beasts for more effort. In the distance the rooftops of Durocornovium were slightly visible and the fields between largely empty of their crops. Falerius ached for an excuse to be away from there and back in his own. Until Fate released him from his obligation, he was going nowhere.

'I want you to meet two friends of mine. Scribonius, Virius, we have a guest joining us. May I introduce Julianus Falerius Silvanus, an ex-centurion of Legio Secunda Augusta.'

'Welcome!' they both echoed from the shelter of the cold plunge pool, two naked bodies with wine cups in their hand. 'Come and join us. The steam is good and the wine full of water too! Slave! Take his clothes!' A slave moved in for further instruction yet discreetly kept his distance.

Falerius felt happy with that and agreed to try the heat of the baths. There wasn't this public facility for many a mile and it was only the preserve of the wealthy to have their own. What better way to relax? The afternoon sun was warm and Falerius needed to escape from recent events. He had worried over Attius and, although the boy's health appeared to be improving it was a distraction from his plans. Nobody could have foreseen such an accident. If the gods willed him to live or die, then so be it. A chance to escape for a brief moment wasn't going to change anything. Falerius slipped out of his tunic, licium and sandals and handed them to the slave to fold away on a shelf. He opened the door of the steam room and tentatively wandered in followed by his two dinner companions. His muscles instantly gave way to the warmth although his mind didn't. Declining the watered wine he would wait until food was prepared so as not to appear undignified, coarse or vulgar. Making a fool of himself before his potential patron could be disastrous for all his ambitions. One of his new friends sidled a little closer raising his drink.

'Falerius, we are interested in this wall that you have built. Tell us a little about it. I hear that it is now the grandest of all structures in the province and the divine Hadrian has decided to protect us from the barbarian for eternity. Is that true?'

Who were these men? Were they agents spying on the unwary or the careless giving away state secrets? What had Helvius told them and what did he know himself? Falerius tried to measure his answer to meet their interest.

'Friends, we have only just met. I am an ex-soldier now turned farmer but what of yourselves?'

Putting the drink down Virius was first to speak. 'I buy wool from Helvius' estates. That wool is taken to Glevum and produces the tunics that the army wear. It provides for their cloaks too. If there is any surplus then I can export it to Gaul where it finds a ready market. It is rough cloth but suitable for the soldiers to wear. I noticed your own cloth Falerius. Fine if I may say so. Where did you buy it?'

'That is a state secret, Virius!' Falerius joked.

Scribonius eyed him up over the rim of his wine cup. 'Friends have no secrets, Falerius. We are all in this together. My luck and wealth is yours too. I have access to funds and could help you. Your son may need to see a doctor? Is that so?'

Falerius could have strung Longinus up there and then. What had he told Cornix about the clay when they were seen talking together at the market in Corinium. What secrets had he given away? Falerius felt trapped but he wasn't a fool. He would hold his tongue until they returned home.

'You asked me about the wall. Our security and prosperity relies solely upon the auxiliaries guarding it at this very moment. Our dead lie within the shadow of its greatness. Britannia is an island as you know but is one wall enough to guard us from our enemies or do we need to build one great wall around us and keep us safe within? That would be too vast to ever be completed and beyond the endurance of any man.'

'Even beyond the endurance of the Divine Emperor Hadrian, Falerius? What say you?' Scribonius posed his question. 'And what of Oceanus? Once, our mighty legions feared to cross its waves. Are there other armies waiting behind us to cross and trap us between the sea and the wall? We could be murdered as we sleep!'

Falerius judged their interest in the subject as self-important and protectionist. Britannia was an island far to the west of the roman world where little happened of consequence. The Emperor had constructed similar barriers throughout Africa and Germania. He was tired of war and wanted the empire to grow in peace without the ever-increasing threat of further taxation to fund his armies. Yet nobody was going to say that. He felt confident of his answer.

'Our legions are ready in their bases of Deva, Eboracum and Isca to defend the province. Our northern front is guarded by auxiliaries and cavalry. The armies of Germania will protect our southern front from such a move that any invader may care to make across the sea and we have our navy. There is no other power in Britannia other than Rome's and the wall is testament to that. You shall both sleep soundly in your beds tonight and for many nights afterwards, as shall your children. Britannia is at peace!'

'Army talk! Friends there are other pleasures about us. Dinner is close to being served. Come!' Helvius returned to gather up his followers like sheep and like sheep they politely obeyed. 'Slave, bring their clothes!' He barked.

Somewhat relaxed and slightly cooled by a rapid immersion in the plunge pool Falerius obeyed his host's instructions and dressed. Helvius had brought out three pairs of soft sandals for them to wear inside the house and thus protect his newly lain mosaic floors. The four of them returned inside and met up with the women, quietly sitting in the shade of a small room painted in red and blue panels, where they had tried to find common ground for conversation. Julia, unlike Falerius, was finding it hard to establish her social standing. She wasn't married, yet wasn't at all unattractive. Her dark hair and strong frame spoke of her native roots. They had land yet not quite enough and Falerius, the soldier having served his time, hadn't quite buttered his way up to any noticeable promotions. Helvius' wife had the measure of her already and appeared politely cold in her promises, via her husband, of further dinner invitations. Julia, silently relieved at this, hoped that Falerius had done better in his early business transactions. At the very least she already wanted to return home.

With accepted authority Helvius stepped forward. 'Guests, please would you join with me in celebrating the Lares before we dine?' Everybody politely followed him to the entrance hall where a small wooden cabinet stood. He opened its doors to reveal inside an array of tiny effigies resembling his deceased family members. Falerius, standing close behind him, felt the lack of a family of his own. His father, like him, had been a soldier and lost his life in one of the many remote battles that combined to win the empire. His body was cremated along with those of his troop. Falerius' mother too was dead, leaving the army as the only family that he had known. Helvius mumbled on before pouring a drop of wine into a small bowl. 'May they live as we do and not want for food or drink in their journey through the Underworld. Pluto protect them!' he concluded leaving the doors open so that the tiny figures could witness the celebrations and not want to stir from their long gone death beds. 'Thank you. Please take your places for dinner.' He clapped his hands and ordered 'music'.

The group returned to the dining room. 'Falerius, I am watching you. Right foot forward into the dining room please,' Helvius asked and he obeyed, unaware of the unlucky significance of the left foot outside the army. Inside the room three couches had been arranged as three sides of a square with the fourth side open to allow slaves to come and go in serving the guests. All other furniture had been removed except for warmth, an iron brazier, silently ticking away in the corner. One slave attended to each table laying the food out in an array of fine bowls for them to pick at. He came and went with fresh dishes and large jugs of wine. Another stood alone in the corner softly playing on a set of panpipes so as not to smother the conversation. Julia and Falerius were shown to their couch, which they shared with Scribonius' wife. Everybody leant forward to pick at the first course before them except Falerius and Julia. Where were their napkins? The first course of smoked fish wrapped in vine leaves came with a rich sauce, and there was muted laughter as food slipped from their greasy fingers.

'Falerius, you have forgotten to bring your napkins!' Helvius spoke from the top table.

'Unfortunately, yes'

'Then please borrow ours and avoid the stains.'

Falerius raised his cup of watered wine as an acknowledgement of thanks to his host. A slave came forward and Julia relaxed. With the table laid with dishes attractively and imaginatively served she could prod away with the small iron knives scattered about for their use. The food was delicious and Helvius boasted that it could not be improved on and that his cook was a man worth holding onto. Not only did he share in his master's tastes but could easily recommend the better wines that were being reserved for later in the meal. What Helvius hadn't boasted about was the mosaic panel in the centre of the room. Its simple geometric interwoven outer pattern was rich in colour – reds, blacks and yellows. Inside, there lay a finer panel depicting Dido and Aeneas. Falerius was drawn to it like the insects drawn to the smoking oil lamps suspended from the ceiling. The two figures were seemingly brought to life by the music, food and conversation of the evening and danced in the light from the lamps playing on the floor. Outside the dining room, wild boar and wolves scavenged through the woods and most people were thinking of their beds.

'Guests, again please pay respect to Eternal Vesta and the spirits of the Penates.' Helvius spoke and, used to obligation, he rose from his couch with a small piece of bread in his hand. Again he uttered his prayers and dropped the offering into the brazier where it smoked gently before rearing up into a small flame and dying out. 'And now the next course,' he triumphantly announced and returned to his couch which he shared with his wife and Scribonius. On the third couch lay Cornix, Virius and his wife. In came the main course of stuffed hare filled with pine kernels, almonds and peppercorns. Over this was poured a hot sauce of dates, spiced wine, onions, mixed with the juices from the cooking pan. On the side dishes the cook had added soft boiled eggs with a honey and pine kernel mix, and a puree of leek and onions. Finally there were mussels to be had served in a sauce of wine and cumin. The warm spicy scent from the dishes rose like the warm steam from the bath house and invited Falerius in. He couldn't refuse.

Throughout the meal Scribonius' wife had politely detailed urban life to an interested Falerius. Since Boudicca's sacking of three Roman towns progress had been remarkable. The enemy, as her husband saw them, were now driven far into the wild mountains of the north and west where they could rot slowly in their straw houses. There wasn't any business to be had there yet the barbarians seemingly envied the wealth they couldn't embrace, for to them it meant slavery and obligation to another. Scribonius secretly admired the military for being resolute in keeping an ever watchful eye over them from the ramparts of their lonely isolated forts. What reward could there ever be for such devotion to duty? What magnificent story of victory over the enemy could arise from the minor skirmishes that were now common place? Where were the pitched battles of old and the generals with their own personal following? Where was the next potential hostile race from which booty and reward could be won once the army had done its job? Not on the island of Britannia. The emperor had decreed that the army had gone far enough in its pursuit of glory and the time had come to stop.

Scribonius' wife confirmed what Falerius had heard earlier in the afternoon – that her husband was a money lender and that they were thriving upon the prosperity spreading throughout the countryside in particular. She was cautious in saying that Helvius too had benefited, asking for loans not only for his own welfare but also that of his public standing in the towns. He had to be seen to be generously promoting the roman way in the form of public buildings and games. It was costing more than his estates could recover and Falerius guessed that most of what his host owned was probably owned by Scribonius too. Hence the constant need for dinner parties, which in their turn added to the expense. The money lender's wife realised that she was probably talking out of turn and decided wisely to change the conversation to Virius, whom they knew as a wool merchant. Falerius relaxed as he realised that they had no connection with the authorities and he was free to speak as he felt without becoming disloyal to the army or the emperor. Virius would tour the larger estates of the wealthy and buy up good supplies of wool. Fashions were slow to arrive in Britannia from Rome but, as Falerius knew, it had only been seven years since the emperor Hadrian had toured the province and that had heralded new patterns in dress and make up. Hadrian himself took to wearing a beard and others quickly followed suit although Falerius chose to shave, as had the other men around the table. The talk idly returned to the towns: the theatres, the ready supply of foodstuffs, the new building projects and of course the ever growing list of new clients wanting to borrow even more money. Scribonius' wife recalled dinner parties in the dingiest of dining rooms where business was being sought and when her husband had returned to conclude matters the old floor had been dug up or overlain with a new mosaic panel. Wealth if it was present was being displayed in full and they were making the most of it; the province recognising that it was finally at peace. Julia, throughout the conversation, maintained that they had only bought a small farm, weren't estate owners and was angry at Falerius warming to another man's wife. He was in fact warming to the life that she was leading. For years he had served on that lonely outpost of the empire not asking for more than his annual pay, and now he wanted to revel in the prosperity his devotion had brought everybody although stopping short of mentioning any loans. On the couch lay the wise old soldier, strong and dependable. On the inside hid the man being seduced by the finer things in life. Rome was weaving its trap.

With their stuffed stomachs, they were thankful that the third course proved lighter and Helvius introduced new entertainments. A dancing girl swayed to the pipe music after which a tutor read verses from classic literature. The conversation too became easier and Falerius had begun to drink the better, stronger wines although he was mindful that they had yet to get home. He picked at the stuffed dates and tried the honey cakes for good measure too before being cajoled into trying a lettuce leaf to aid his digestion and give him sleep. He could see Julia trying hard to suppress a yawn and asked Helvius for their leave.

'Falerius, of course! Forgive me I haven't spoken much with you this evening. Maybe we could conclude a business arrangement at another date? I will have a slave accompany you as far as you wish him to go and may you travel safely through the dark. Farewell!'

Both Julia and Falerius politely said their goodbyes to the other guests and returned their sandals and napkins. Before leaving the villa Falerius couldn't help being drawn to another mosaic again dancing in the light of a dying oil lamp. It depicted the four seasons with two panels clearly visible showing in one a naked Spring dancing, whilst in the other Winter clad in a cloak held up a twig and a dead hare. Once out of earshot the slave revealed that Helvius had been a keen sportsman although those days had been brought to an end by an injury in the chase. He liked to portray himself as he was then and this vanity had shone throughout the house. He was often away on business, the slave added, although he thoroughly enjoyed being at home. As for a man amongst other men, Helvius liked to surround himself with those he could intimidate and bully. The slave then cut himself off for fear of being repeated. He needn't have worried for a grateful Falerius thanked him for his honesty and he wouldn't be saying any more on the subject. They parted shortly before his boundary and the slave, so as not to be caught up in the clearing away of the dinner party, showed no hurry in being off.

Julia waited for her moment with the slave having gone and his torch an ever smaller light in the distance. 'Have you secured our future?' she asked.

'No,' answered Falerius. 'I thought that we could talk in the bath house but Helvius left me with his guests and went off with Cornix. Maybe he will return tomorrow with a proposition but without having given over this land there is little more I could have done. The evening became a celebration of pleasure rather than of business,' he answered smugly. 'Also think of Cominius.'

'Yes, of course,' she replied before silently going indoors.

The following day brought with it no sign of Gaius Helvius Bonus or his bailiff, Cornix. Instead the skies brought with them an unexpected early winter hue of lead and from them fell rain just as hard. Falerius stared at the road willing the magistrate to appear but he knew that only the hardiest would be out travelling in this weather. What offering to which god would seal the business that yesterday appeared so easy? His mood wasn't helped by Longinus returning from the fields complaining that digging was useless as the ditches were filling with water as quickly as he could dig them out. The land was saturated and would be good for nothing. The clay was far too wet and only massive investments in timber would dry it out ready for crushing. Falerius had to concede defeat and abandon the endeavour until the New Year when the fields would naturally drain. Winter was going to be eked out on his savings and what remained from the wool sales. However in this time of quiet he could plan and think about what to do.

'Longinus; a moment. Come here! What were you discussing with Cornix outside the market at Corinium?'

'Nothing, Master, except that he was once a slave too and we had something in common.' Falerius burst into laughter. 'To think that anybody could trust their slave with anything and to become something! Get on with your work.' Longinus duly trudged off pulling his broad hat over his head and tugging his cloak tightly around him in an attempt to avoid the rain.

One more day led to a month of days passing and still there was no sign of Helvius. Falerius discounted that he was waiting for a return dinner invitation as his house was not worthy of that honour. Was Scribonius waiting for him to ask for a loan and in return he would snatch the land? His fingers itched as they turned a silver denarius over and over in their grasp until there was a real danger of the emperor's head being worn from the precious coin. He put it down and concentrated on his plans instead. There would be a mosaic panel on his floor and fine painted plaster panels on his walls. He would employ an excellent cook and offer copious invitations to his friends to dine. If he had to accept patronage then it would be on his terms only and they were that the farm had to remain in Attius' name when he died and in that there was no negotiating. Falerius would continue with mining the clay and sell his wool for its inflated price on quality and with the profit he would buy out Cominius' stake. To win a successful battle Falerius planned to outwit and out-manoeuvre his enemy but at that very moment the enemy had refused to show.

Winter dragged on and the family's costs rose. There was oil for the lamps, warm clothing and stout boots for them all. Food was short and the snows were making obtaining fresh supplies difficult. A new crop of anything was a long way off and the diet ground on with salted meats and pickled vegetables. Falerius dreamt of being back at Helvius' table enjoying the fruits of his enigmatic business dealings. It all seemed so easy to a desperate man. You give me what I want and I will give you a little of what you want in return. He could feast forever in Bacchus' company.

Attius broke into his dream. 'Father when I can ride again?'

'Apologies, son.'

'When can I ride again?' he repeated. 'My head has stopped hurting and I no longer feel faint. The bright sunshine hurts my eyes but I want to go out. I'm tired of staying indoors.'

'We can go out now if you want, little soldier. It looks like the snow is going to stop and there is blue sky beyond. Before darkness falls I need to check the ditches and make sure that the fields aren't filling with water. You can come with me if you like but it will be cold.' The boy didn't mind and enjoyed being about the farm with his father. Since his accident Longinus had kept his distance although Falerius, whilst threatening to do so, hadn't punished him. To have avoided the expense and obligation of taking his son to the doctor Falerius was grateful. The gods had willed it and without question he had accepted their gift.

'Is Spring to return, Father?'

'Yes and naked too!' laughed Falerius. 'Come on, let's go.'

It was on one of these father and son journeys around the small fields that the magistrate appeared with Cornix in tow. Falerius thought of the dinner party and the tale of Persephone who, in returning to the blue skies of Demeter for half the year took the land out of its sterile winter sleep and allowed the crops to ripen and grow. Was this an omen?

'Falerius, greetings!' he cried from his horse with the warmth of the sun upon his back.

'My greetings to you and to you too, Cornix. How are you?'

They were both well. Helvius in his diplomatic manner apologised for the delay in returning and explained that they had made no plans for a meeting again at dinner and in any case he had been extremely busy if not wholly inconvenienced by the bad weather himself. Falerius thought a moment on what he had just said. They had made no plans for meeting again. If this was patronage then Helvius wasn't winning Falerius over. 'What brings you out here?' he asked. 'I thought I would take the time to put a proposition to you and maybe Cornix could look over your land,' he replied.

'What kind of proposition?' asked Falerius.

Helvius dismounted and handed the reins to Cornix. 'Come aside,' he beckoned.

'Attius, return to your mother and ask for drinks. There is beer in the house. Now run along.' The boy eagerly ran off pleased with the responsibility of an errand from his father.

'Falerius, I have had the time to think. I wish to make you an offer to buy your land. It will be at a fair price and allow you to stay and farm it for me under the responsibility of Cornix here. Your wool is excellent and Virius has been finding me reliable buyers in Londinium who will pay a good price. In addition I will provide you with an annual payment that if you save well over the years could mean you buying another farm elsewhere.'

What had Longinus really been discussing with Cornix at the market?

The magistrate continued. 'We believe your secret to be in the soil. I've made enquiries of Virius and he tells me that other wool producers further east and north of Londinium dig up a clay that makes cleaning their fleeces easier. Is this what you are doing Falerius and does anybody know?' Did anybody who could tax him know?

'You have dug a lot of ditches,' added Cornix from the vantage point of his mount.

'The land is wet, you know it is!'

They seemed to have him cornered and ready for the kill. Falerius fought back. 'Magistrate, I may have asked for time to consider your offer but the answer is that I will not sell the land. It is not entirely mine to sell. Neither would I wish to become a tenant of yours. Is that enough for you?' he argued.

'Falerius my friend, come. I understand. All my other tenants have thought as you do but have seen the wisdom of my way. Your son could be educated and your house rebuilt. You could enjoy a comfortable life and not want for anything. On the other hand I could stop buying your wool and advise Virius to do the same. Your market, Falerius, would disappear and your farm become worthless. You would be begging me to buy it then but at a much lower price than I am offering you. Don't be a fool!'

Falerius knew no greater fury than he was experiencing now. 'You had better be off before I chase you off,' he threatened, unconcerned by Helvius' true authority that could have seen him in trouble.

'Farewell then Falerius, and good luck!' Helvius spat out, remounting via a small hummock and turning to face the way he had apparently come.

In their leaving Attius returned and noticed the distress in his father's face. 'Mother said to bring your friends into the house for a drink. She has cleaned a little for them. Why are they leaving?' Falerius couldn't find it in his heart to tell the boy the truth. The farm was going to be his even if it killed him.

CHAPTER VI

WHO TO TRUST

'Master Cominius, there is a visitor at the east gate looking for you. Am I permitted to ask the guards to allow him in?'

'Who is it, Marcus?' Cominius said. He was watching a small group of soldiers idly gambling outside, their cheers breaking the boredom of sound amongst the barrack blocks.

'Falerius; your friend the sheep farmer.'

'Oh! The watchword is 'Audax', Marcus. Bring him in.' Cominius went back to his gambling and upon a wax tablet he had written the word STULTUS without thought. Within a few moments Marcus was there with Falerius by his side. Cominius closed the wooden pages containing the wax and returned it and the stylus to the desk. 'Thank you Marcus. You may leave us,' he said.

'Falerius, a surprise visit! Am I due some money?' The two men clasped hands and embraced. It had been many years since they had last seen one another. 'You can't have too many years left to serve?' Falerius enquired. 'Not many,' Cominius replied not wishing to court any bad luck. 'I try to keep away from the trouble and let the younger men take the risks. They seem more than willing if there is any danger. In fact it is so quiet that sometimes they look for trouble. A dangerous game to play! I am saving my energies for my retirement,' he added, thrusting his groin backwards and forwards. They both laughed out aloud although behind the smiles Falerius wished him far better luck than he had had.

'Can I offer you some food or drink? Please sit down. How are Julia and your son? Has there been a problem?' Falerius felt himself being interrogated. 'Yes. Pour a drink and I will tell you about it,' he said. Falerius felt like changing the subject and as he had instantly felt at home amongst the leather, wood and steel smells coming from the slightly stale air of Cominius' room, the military seemed a good diversion. 'I've seen a few new faces in here and heard a few new languages as well,' he quipped. The cold stone walls of the fortress had once again embraced him in the cloak of human warmth and again he had felt safe from the seemingly hostile world outside.

'You were fortunate to find me here, Falerius. In a day or so I am to go west again and continue the surveying of roads towards a new town, Moridunum. The Silures are now looking for a peaceful settlement to our wars and we of course are looking for a peaceful way of continuing to take their gold mines!' Cominius was safe in telling this to his friend. He added that there was to be an armed escort eighty men strong and that on their way west they had to call in at the auxiliary forts quietly nestled at river and valley junctions. 'We're not expecting any trouble, for the spies and scouts have done their work, but I just want to get there and back safely.'

'How long will you be gone?' a worried Falerius asked.

'It depends whether the auxiliaries are still at their post or not.'

'Hasn't the wall swallowed them all up?' Falerius tried to joke and without unduly worrying his friend whom he was now seeing as a coward. 'The wall itself has enraged the barbarians but too far north for us to be concerned with.' Cominius had a good grasp of the current military situation regarding the province and that comforted Falerius somewhat. 'The barbarians complain of the taxes to pass through the wall but most of all they dislike it for it has split the tribes in two.'

'Divide and rule, the noble roman way in war, Cominius.'

'Unfortunately it may well become divide and unite for as you know the emperor Hadrian had forbidden any more campaigning beyond its limit except for routine patrols. How do we know therefore what they are planning in their mountain retreats?' His cowardice again shone through.

'The legions are all in their fortresses at Deva and Eboracum are they not?'

'They are,' Cominius confirmed, 'but what of the quality now the fighting has stopped? They'd be better off being drawn away to fight elsewhere before they and the island fall asleep in idleness!' Cominius poured himself a cup of wine and offered the same across the table to Falerius. 'Maybe that's what the Picts are waiting for?'

He went on to make a snoring noise and claimed that although the army of Britannia had done its work there was still plenty left for him to do. It was a quiet life but not without the occasional incident. 'We lost four cavalrymen last week. The weather suddenly got worse whilst out on a patrol and they fell into a ravine. We left their bodies there,' he added for interest. Many soldiers would meet their deaths in that way deprived of the glory of battle or the aggression of having thrown a spear at the enemy. Falerius felt the old loyalties returning and yearned to be a younger man once more.

Cominius stopped looking at the bottom of his cup and turned to his friend who was still, in his mind, fighting long finished battles and it showed on his face. 'Come, Falerius. What is the real reason for your visit? I could talk military matters all day but you haven't travelled this far to do so yourself.' He waited patiently for an answer.

'Our deal, my friend, the one where you have a share in the land. I may require you to change the agreement.'

'In what way?'

'In the way that you offer to buy out my share and own the farm yourself. I will then offer to farm it for you until better times. I would not want too much in return for my half.' Falerius went on to explain about mining the clay and using it as Cominius had dictated. The quality was poor however and the reserves limited. Falerius had thought that there were better seams under the land of his neighbour. 'Then make him an offer,' Cominius confidently announced. 'We could raise the money. Ask him.' The neighbour being Gaius Helvius Bonus.

'I've had poor sales of wool and with having to take it further to other markets in Calleva for example, there hasn't been enough profit. The army too are offering low prices in Corinium and new large estates are growing all the time. The competition is becoming harder and I am getting into financial trouble,' Falerius explained. 'Then how can me buying the land help you for the problem would only become mine,' Cominius probed. 'Yes, but the demand for good land is growing as people choose to come here for the island's riches and they wish to live outside the towns.'

'The land is wet, Falerius. We both know that. It isn't good land.'

'Durocornovium is growing little by little as people invest in it. There are the roads north and south. New ways of doing things are being introduced and the farm will be your pension to come.'

'And what of your pension, Falerius? How do you plan to spend that or have you already spent it and hence the visit?'

'My body aches,' confessed Falerius. 'You are younger than me. I cannot tell Julia for she will worry and with each day that passes I can only pray that my son becomes a man quickly so as to look after us. He is all I have.'

'And your savings?'

'Nearly all gone.'

Cominius looked hard at his business partner, the man who had once saved his life. 'You owe me nothing Falerius,' he said. 'But by the same token I have provided you with an opportunity for you to use. I cannot simply allow it to fail. Finds of other precious metals and minerals are now becoming harder to keep quiet as the peace has enabled tribesmen to sell their lands to the emperor. We are encouraged not to take by force that which we could pay a small price for.' He emphasised the word small. 'That of course has limited my opportunities. I was relying upon you as a trusted friend to do well!' Cominius silently poured two more cups of wine, the very noise of it disturbing him as it fell into the empty vessels. He spilt a drop on the table and swore. 'What are we going to do, Falerius? What are we going to do?' he bitterly repeated.

The two men once fighting in war now were separated in the peace that followed it. In that room Cominius was the first to broker a treaty.

'Falerius, listen,' he said, 'return to your farm and continue as you have done. I know that it is going to be a struggle to survive but I will lend you a little more money. I may be able to persuade the army to buy a few more of your skins but there are only so many bribes that can go unnoticed. I have to leave for western Siluria soon and then all will be out of my hands. We have been promised peace for all these years now but who knows? A stronger vexillation is going to cover the ground between us and Deva to protect our flanks and then there is always the temporary safety of the forts providing their auxiliaries are at their posts and not moved north to the wall. I am confident that all the planning is correct and that I will safely return in four month's time. After that I will have to come out in person and visit. Marcus can draw up a report in the meantime. I'm sorry Falerius, but that is the best that I can offer you.'

Falerius' strength and courage were deserting him and therefore this was a peace agreement that he required more than Cominius. Many years ago he had picked up a sword in the same way that his father had but Falerius didn't want to die penniless, broken and used by the state. Attius would inherit the farm, his own debts would be settled with Cominius and his own final journey through the Underworld made easier by his actions now. Falerius would not become a debtor and there would be, on no account, any selling of the land to Gaius Helvius Bonus. If he had to wait the four months then he would.

Cominius accompanied his friend to the gate in the same way that he had seen him off all those years ago at his discharge. How the circumstances had changed and how difficult farming beyond the safety of the fortress walls was proving. A military reputation counted for nothing out there except to recall past glories somewhere with somebody. The two men embraced and then parted.

'Until four months, Falerius. Until then, farewell!'

He watched the gaunt frame of a man fifty years old amble away into the ill disciplined streets of the vicus. Gone was the military gait of the soldier and instead Falerius wore the laurel leaf worries of the world about his head. Cominius had expected his friend to be growing fat off the land, dining at sumptuous tables and being heard in the market squares around. The truth was a different story and Cominius felt that Falerius had lied to him. The farmer was hiding a secret that would cause him to waste away even further, as if disease-stricken and helpless. Wanting to look no further he turned for his room, his papers and his plans. In passing the soldiers still gambling, one of them cried out that they had beaten the crooked dice and won. A fight broke out rapidly quelled by two burly guards.

Falerius' own mood on the journey home was somehow lightened by Cominius' actions. He would stop at the nearest wayside shrine and offer thanks for his friend. Not having enough in the way of money for a magnanimous gesture, Falerius hoped that he had enough to persuade Fortuna to bring his friend safely back from the dangers of Siluria. At such a shrine, set a little way back off the roadside and marked by a simply carved stone altar Falerius asked the goddess if she were listening. He kept his face lowered and was meticulous in his delivery in offering up a gift in return for reward. 'I willingly serve you,' he muttered before breaking away from that divine space, his eyes to the ground. Only the open sky, the woods and the creatures that scurried across the road bore witness to the humbling of Julianus Falerius Silvanus, once centurion of Legio Secunda Augusta. The rites solemnly over, he made for home.

Julia was in the garden when Falerius arrived. The year had been a good one up to then and the plants that she had selected were beginning to show their value in the coming months. There would be no shortage of fruit or vegetables, barring disease. Even if the old house required the odd roof tile replacing or the daub walls repairing they would eat well and hopefully have enough to save for the winter which was a long way off. The soil in her garden was easy to work when dry, and in his absence Longinus had done a good job in clearing the weeds and turning it over. The orchards, pruned back in the winter, now bore the fruit of heavy blossom and the firewood pile was full and drying out in the warm midday sun. His stock looked healthy and the small rectangular fields were not too riddled with weeds either. He had always liked it like this; the small farm looking after its own, standing on its own two feet in simplicity. If he could have done, then he would have chosen to grow cereals for there is always a need to eat, whereas fashions and new clothes alike are fickle; they come and go. Yet he wasn't too displeased with what he had been given, although the ditches where clay extraction had begun were now overgrown and hid their recent past beneath a canopy of green nettles deterring anybody from venturing further. His wealth still lay beneath his feet. It couldn't be stolen and neither could it go anywhere. That empowered him, lifted his spirits and Falerius vowed not to worry any further about the subject of the clay. He walked into the garden.

'Welcome home. The gods protect you!' Julia kissed him and then held him close before looking him over like a stranger. 'I've only been gone a number of days,' Falerius said, 'Little has changed in me except that I am growing the emperor's beard.' He rubbed his chin in mockery of the new fashion. 'You appear happier. Cominius must have seen you?' she added.

'Yes, he did see me,' Falerius went on, explaining that he had only told him as much as he felt he needed to know about the situation. He hadn't mentioned Gaius Helvius Bonus or the offer to buy the farm. 'Cominius is away for four months in the west but when he returns in the autumn he will pay us a visit and we can tell him the truth. Julia . . .' Falerius' voice changed, causing her to stop what she was doing. 'Being back at Isca Silurum made me think. I don't belong here as much as I think I do. If we could, would you return there with me and we could settle alongside the other veterans and farm? There would always be the security for you and it is a way of life that we have all known, even Attius. We would be accepted back and there are still people alive that I knew. I have seen them! My reputation will count for something.' He sounded excited. 'Think about it, will you?' That was a shock for Julia. Was the old warrior accepting the inevitable, accepting defeat? 'Has Helvius beaten us? Has he truly driven us away from our lands? Of course I will follow you anywhere,' she added with a tear in her eye. 'If that is your wish then, yes.' She went inside and returned quickly with something in her hand. Falerius was staring at the far horizon lost in thought. 'You must read this. Cornix has been out to deliver this letter.' She passed over the thin wooden pages sealed in wax for him to read. 'Did he say anything?' Falerius felt the natural aggression in his voice rising. 'Has he made any threats?'

'No,' Julia quietly assured him. Falerius broke open the seal and turned the thin page to reveal the scrawled message written in black ink.

From G Helvius Bonus to J Falerius Silvanus. Greetings. Please accept my apologies for our disagreements. Would you accompany me upon a journey to Aquae Sulis on business with your son.

We can end hostilities in a most agreeable way. I await your reply.

A cloud drifted across the face of the sun and Aeolus lifted the pink and white blossom from the trees. The white horse on the hillside was momentarily darker in colour as a shadow passed over it; the spring and stream sounded closer than ever.

'Oh Fortuna, what have I done?' whispered Falerius momentarily struck down by an involvement in actions beyond his control. The shades between the trees were no longer an unexplained darkness but simply a shadow as was his upon the ground he stood upon. 'Atoms,' he continued silently whispering to himself. 'Atoms and nothing more.' He gazed at the thin page of writing expecting the answer to the question to reveal itself there and then. 'Falerius, come inside. You are looking tired. He will not expect an answer today so come and rest.' Julia had noticed the sudden change of character and was worried. He had always respected the gods and paid his dues, for the army and state had expected it, but privately Falerius had sought their favour when it suited. 'What,' Julia wondered, 'had he asked for?'

Eventually his temper burst out. 'He must think me a fool! The meal, his manners, he can keep them all! I owe him nothing. We have managed without his interference this far and I know times have been hard but he cannot control me in this way. Cominius is with us now and he will be back shortly so my answer is 'No'.' The anger flashed across his eyes from deep within. He threw the thin pages tied by a string hinge into the wind where they were momentarily carried before settling like a bird, wings outstretched, onto the nettle canopy over the ditch. 'Has he cleared his lists of people to persecute and starting afresh? Is he mocking me?'

'No, he is not mocking you,' Julia said, quietly approaching Falerius and taking his arm. 'Where is Aquae Sulis and why offer to take you there?' A subdued Falerius explained that it was a town to the west of them, famous within the island for its natural hot waters that were once sacred to the Celtic god Sulis. 'People go there looking to be healed by sacred Minerva,' he added. 'Does he think me ill enough to require healing?' Falerius' anger flared again at the fact that the Magistrate was not there to receive it personally. 'Have the time to bathe every day like he does . . . in luxury or do I want to have the skin of a woman?' He mocked. 'The only illness that I have is . . .' and he stopped.

'What illness? You haven't spoken to me about anything,' Julia was cross about the silences that were now opening up. 'What is it that you are keeping from me, Falerius?' she begged to know.

'There are pains. The pains that come from years of marching and fighting; all soldiers suffer from them. I had hopes for a quiet life in the warmth of the fields to end my days and not of the fighting that is going on now. If I can rest then I am sure to recover, the gods willing.'

'Then why not take the opportunity that he is giving to you? If the waters heal, then they can heal you too. Wealth doesn't matter and with Attius with you, there will be safe company. All you need to do is keep your wits about you and do not offer what you do not have. Falerius, if it heals you then please go.' She made it sound simple and attractive. A woman that was tired herself. 'I will keep Longinus here just in case it is a trick and Cornix returns to seize the farm in your absence. How many days will you be gone?' Falerius thought it to be five at the most. 'Let's find Attius,' he said.

Predictably the boy was to be found with the slave. His duties were mainly over for the day and Attius had taken advantage of it in the form of wanting to practice his swordplay. In his right hand he clutched a wooden gladius and eagerly stabbed at Longinus who was just as eagerly avoiding the thrusts.

'Attius.'

'Father, you're back!' The boy dropped his weapon and ran to clutch his father's arms where he was lifted high into the air. 'A soldier now, eh? Whatever happened to the cavalryman? Were you bored or is it safer not falling from a horse?'

'No, father. Cavalry training was this morning!'

Falerius caught Longinus' gaze looking down to the ground in submission but forgave him easily as the farm was looking as tidy as ever and he had been working hard. 'Longinus isn't a real soldier, father, can you teach us both?' Attius asked. 'We'll have to see. First I have been asked to go on a journey and would you like to come with me. You can ride Roma. Do you feel fit enough? It is a long way.' Falerius watched the boy's face light up. He was fit and ready for anything. Since Roma's kick he had recovered well and knew what to avoid in bringing on a recurrence of the symptoms. As long as the sun wasn't too bright or the day's riding too hard then he would be fine. His father had to protect him from extreme tiredness and stop if his son said so. Other than that there wouldn't be a problem and it had been a while since they had travelled together and this wasn't business; or was it? 'Where are we going, father?' he asked.

'You'll find out.'

So Falerius and his son dutifully reported to the house south of Durocornovium on the allotted day and at the allotted time. There they were met by Helvius' groom who was to accompany them on the journey. The morning dew was far from being lifted by the warming power of the sun and two trails followed their footsteps across the grass. They had given their animals to the groom who in loosening the girths allowed the animals to briefly rest whilst everybody else made ready to leave. Helvius was to be found sitting at a table beneath the porticoed entrance eating a small breakfast. Falerius thought that he looked out of place wearing a simple woollen tunic and leather breeches but this was a journey to be made on horseback and he didn't want to suffer any more discomfort than was really necessary. Cornix had predicted the weather was going to be good for the foreseeable future and they wouldn't encounter any problems in travelling. It would be light and fast.

An apologetic Helvius rose from his seat. 'Falerius, forgive me. My actions have brought shame upon myself and you must think me cruel.' Out of the corner of his eye Falerius noticed the magistrate's wife within listening distance, but she soon quietly slipped away. 'This must be your son?' Helvius enquired. 'Have you recovered from your accident, boy? I am pleased to see you with your father and hope that you both enjoy the journey.'

'Where are we going?' Attius asked in excitement.

'Aquae Sulis, boy! Aquae Sulis.' It meant nothing at all.

The two adults finished their polite conversations and soon were ready with Tancorix, the groom, bringing up the rear with a spare pony carrying clothes and a little food and drink. Helvius' plan was not to travel directly south picking up the west road where it dissected the road from Corinium to Venta Belgarum but instead they would travel along a shorter route over the hills on a track just as good and quicker. They would then meet the west road at a place where it crossed a river and near a strange hill that appeared to have been made by human hands long before the Romans had arrived in the island. There they could rest and water their mounts before continuing. It was going to be a beautiful day as Cornix had predicted with the rising sun peeling back the clouds to reveal a bright blue sky. The ground beneath their hooves was soft, and without stones, Helvius and Falerius vied for the position of who was the better horseman as they cantered on. They pulled up to allow the other two to catch them and Falerius commented on the magistrate's riding skills. He himself had ridden in the army and Helvius, in admitting that his hunting days were over, nevertheless still liked to keep his balance as he called it. 'Once on top of the hill we can talk,' he said before cantering off again. Eventually the ground before them rose too steeply and they slowed to a walk. The shoulders of the five animals worked hard to pull themselves and their loads high above the countryside below and were rewarded with a rest at the top. Falerius felt as relaxed as he had done for a long time and allowed Helvius to point out the directions that they would be travelling in, plus any landmarks that they could see. The road was about ten miles distant Helvius stated and without milestones they would have to guess at their progress. For both men that wasn't a problem, for Helvius travelled a lot on business and Falerius had marched along most of the roads between here and the far north. Nobody spoke for a little while as their thoughts were carried over the ridge by the wind and far into the distance. Helvius was the first.

'Is everybody ready? Shall we continue?' This time the pace was at a walk and with the ever rising sun all four of them could see far off without obstruction. An occasional abandoned hill-fort would come into view and Attius begged to be allowed to break off and discover its secrets before rejoining the party. The two groups slowly separated with Helvius and his guest taking to the front, the horses finding the going easy and pleased at their work. The farmer was within hearing of everything that Helvius said.

'Falerius, Cornix tells me that you have stopped digging the earth. Is it true? Do you fear the tax collectors?'

'I have nothing to dig for Helvius. You alone ought to know that!' and he laughed. 'You have taken away my market and therefore my reason for wanting to work any harder than I have to. We can get by.' He tried hard to suppress the anger boiling below but this was a pleasure trip and business could wait another day. Falerius played with the reins in his hands and stretched his legs straight out from the saddle to ward off any aches. Looking to the right he tried to avoid too much contact with Helvius' face.

'And do you understand my invitation today, Falerius?' Helvius went on.

Falerius had to think hard. The memories of the dinner party, the refusal to sell his land and the subsequent fall in his fortunes all came rushing back. They had come from an invitation. This time he would offer a more measured response. 'Yes, Helvius,' he simply said, 'this beautiful land, this fine weather and an opportunity to bathe in the waters of Minerva. A chance to indulge myself for which I thank you.'

'Good, Falerius. I am pleased, that at last we finally understand one another. I shall ask nothing more.'

Falerius too was pleased that the conflict was apparently over and maybe there could be some thawing in their personal relationship and business dealings. He questioned Helvius about the current markets for good quality wool and wasn't surprised to learn that he had tried to source the clay from the east but the cost of transport had made it impossible. It was also too far out of Helvius' sphere of influence to make it feasible to buy land there or rent it. Other people were already exploiting the mineral find whether he liked it or not. Helvius also let slip that his financial supporter Scribonius had already had meetings with new potential clients out there and as he had the additional cost of new urban projects to bear, then Helvius couldn't risk losing that money and backing to somebody else. It was in his interest to obtain a deal with Falerius and the soldier sensed a new weakness in the man. Virius couldn't be trusted either, as his personal fortune depended upon others, namely Scribonius.

'Let us forget business, Falerius. Mercury can wait a day or two I'm sure. Let the Fates serve us as they choose and enjoy ourselves.'

With the hilltop track now descending into a green verdant river valley, Falerius could see the road ahead as Helvius had stated. It appeared from nowhere, met the river, forded it with ease and then continued on in its relentless course into the west. Dots of people were moving slowly along it. Falerius could also make out the strange hill that had been mentioned. It stood out alone and resembled none of the hills that surrounded it whilst there, slightly to the north of the hill stood an even stranger circle of enormous stones not crafted from human hands. How had the Celts managed this and yet lost their kingdom? If Falerius was fascinated then so too was his son, who was ever eager to be off and exploring the new landscape before him. They were indeed strange sights in an even stranger island. He pulled on his reins and made the horse ready for the downhill walk, as the hillsides were steep and without grip. The others did the same. With the party stopped for a rest and food, the two men went to climb the strange hill whilst Tancorix was left to prepare the food and see to the mounts. Attius chose to look around the small market that had established itself at a convenient point where a fresh water supply was readily available. He was attracted to the ramshackle collection of stalls offering for sale food produce, pots and religious tokens. Buyers could also be tempted to part with their money by more stalls selling leather goods and other artefacts that were emanating from the new towns growing either end of the road and in between. The fingers of commerce were spreading deep out into the countryside as an advertisement for all that was good in the Romans being there. However there weren't too many people buying and the day was becoming hotter. A lazy heat haze danced across the fields and the canopies barely stirred in a breathless sky. Attius was instead drawn to the glass coolness of the small river, swift flowing and clad on either side by reeds. The shingle road surface met it and then disappeared beneath the surface on a flagstone bed and then reappeared again as shingle again on the opposite bank. Trails of water left a mark of the last cart to have crossed through it rapidly drying in the heat. The clear water swirled in pools of light as it flowed over the road and Attius, watching from the banks noticed the occasional traveller drop an offering into the waters without stopping and without ceremony or any acknowledgement for the gift. At the first opportunity and when the road was quiet he sidled down to the crossing to see what it was that people were dropping into the cool waters. Glinting in the bottom of the river bed and not yet covered by the constant shifting of its course lay a few coins freshly offered up. He took his sandals off and waded in, surprised by the cold and mesmerised by the green waving weeds in the current. Looking about him he could see in the distance the twin figures of his father and Helvius standing on the hill. His feet moved in the gravel as something brushed against them and Attius quickly thrust his right arm into the murky waters, grabbed something and then pulled it out. The smooth silt continued to flow across his toes and then the water cleared to reveal the river bed. The sun shone like diamonds upon its surface and there was no sound.

Once back on the bank Attius opened his hand to see what he had in it. It felt weighty and was a grey silver colour although clearly not a coin. The metal had been carefully folded upon itself and Attius unrolled it just as carefully. Blowing the silt away and wiping it clean he could make out the letters and words that spelt CURSED ARE YOU THAT STEAL FROM ME. He didn't understand it and carefully rolled it up again before returning it to the deepest part of the river with a plop. In the distance his father and Helvius were now climbing down from the hill and the wood smoke that gently drifted across the fields denoted food. He quickly waded in again, bent down and sorted the gravel and silt between his fingers until he found a coin. It was brown with age and well worn. With distain Attius again returned this one to the river with a plop, got out, replaced his sandals and trudged off for lunch.

'Have you been enjoying yourself son?' Falerius could see that he had been in the water. 'Have you watered the animals?' he said.

'No,' Attius replied, but he would. Then with horses seen to, a light stew and bread for lunch washed down with a sweet honey-drink everybody was eager to be off. The road would rise again leaving the small market and river far behind before plunging again and meeting their overnight stop.

The following morning dawned bright and clear. All four ached from the previous day's exertions and the straw mattresses of the small beds had added to their general stiffness. Falerius stretched himself and yawned as he walked out into the small yard where the horses and ponies had been groomed by Tancorix prior to having their saddles and bridles fitted. The air was cool and filled his ageing lungs without too much trouble and coughing. Helvius and Attius vied for the last to be up, both walking out with food in their hands or mouths. Past the wooden gated entrance to the small mansio, pilgrims were already on the road to Aquae Sulis, walking as if in a trance like state towards their ultimate destination and the healing powers of the magic waters. 'It's a shorter ride today,' Helvius proclaimed, 'I think we will arrive late morning if the road isn't too busy with these long lost vagrants.' He was scathing towards the ghost like figures out so early and dismissive of their searching for something to believe in. 'They'd be better off dying at home,' he said. Helvius slipped easily into his saddle and made himself comfortable taking the reins in his left hand ready for the off. Falerius and Attius followed suit by leaping off the mounting block into their saddles. Only Tancorix remained to mount up and this he did with practiced ease, the reins of the lead pony clutched securely in his hand. The party took to the road and headed off west following the ghost like figures as they went. To avoid running them down, this not being amongst the widest of roads in the province, Helvius took to riding on the cleared strip of land that ran parallel to the road on either side. The motley collection of souls was safe for the time being and if they lived long enough could be sure of making their destination later that day. The milestones soon tallied up and the horses were keen for their work in the clear morning air.

Fifteen, ten, eight, seven and then four miles, the west road approached them and joined with the great road running north east to south west from Isca Dumnoniorum to Lindum where Helvius stopped to give his mount a rest and to admire the views. The beast, its flanks pushing in and out against his legs, stood motionless except to turn its head to see where the others were. Its head, lowered again slightly to take in more air, looked forward, its ears alert for any sound, its eyes fixed on the far horizon. A smell of warm sweat rose from its damp skin and flecks of white bubbled around its girth. 'All downwards from here,' Helvius shouted to the last in the group. That was Falerius. 'There she is: the beautiful town below us of Aquae Sulis.' In the valley below a small settlement was spreading, although dominated at the present by one group of buildings only, namely the baths. Another river could be seen barely moving and on the far horizon this same road was seen making its inevitable way towards the south west.

'Forget not, Roman, that it is your special genius to rule the peoples,' Helvius quoted with an air of noble pride. 'Unfortunately you have killed them all in the north, Falerius, and so I have to come here to conduct my business instead. Talk and rumour, they make for good business and as you've had your share of slave booty and war chests then it's my turn to profit from what is left in this glorious island. Empire without limit,' he went on, whilst more pilgrims in dirty dusty tunics passed them couching their heads to listen to the strange plump man and his orations from horseback. From the north smaller groups of soldiers joined the gathering swarm looking for relief from their wounds and keen to believe the stories that had brought them there too. The cult of Minerva deserved her status. Helvius could smell the fortunes here as Falerius could his in the clay, pee and sheep oils back home. 'What are your plans, Helvius?' Falerius asked. 'There must be enough merchants here to fill the great baths themselves.'

'Obviously, Falerius. But look around you. The grand houses of the rich sit upon these hills, their owners looking for the best in garments. These pilgrims, filthy from their travels across the empire will require clothing before the cold of winter disrupts their journeys home, and the very priests squatting down there in their dark temples all require clothing. Where is it going to come from Falerius? Open your eyes to opportunity.' Attius was full of questions too and didn't hesitate to ask if the Britons would want their land back at some time if it was so full of riches. 'Won't the emperor come here to live?' he asked the orator simply.

'The great emperor, boy, has already been and in your father's time too. He has seen these riches and ensured that they are all locked away behind his wall for us to share. His empire is vast and he himself has work to do elsewhere. He won't be back. So enjoy yourself whilst you can!'

'Father, have I a special genius inside me?' Attius wanted answering. 'I'll explain as we ride down the hill.' Falerius, as briefly as he could, recalled the story of Aeneas the True and his flight from Troy, a great city in the far east and a long way from where they were at that moment. In his escape the warrior took his father and son with him but the old man died on the way to their eventual home, Italia. With the support of favourable gods and after many epic struggles Aeneas finally established a new kingdom where his son was destined to rule. He recalled showing his son the wolf on the back of an old coin to further add to the story.

'Did he have a queen like Caesar had Cleopatra?'

'He did have a queen, son, but he had to leave her behind on the advice of the gods and that caused many years fighting for the Romans against their bitter enemies – Carthage.'

'Why were the gods fighting?' Attius asked innocently.

'You ask too many questions. I will explain it more when we have time on the way home.' Falerius knew that his son's enquiring mind could benefit from Helvius' offer of a tutor for him. His own knowledge had come from camp talk, the symbols he had seen painted on ceremonial shields, and simple mosaics that were now springing up boasting of their owner's love for the classics even if they had never studied them. All these stories made up an empire and that was what was special about it to him. He certainly felt special as he rode towards the first of the houses they met on the edge of the town. A temple grew in stature before him sitting squat on its podium of an earthen bank. Steps led up to the entrance darkened by the lack of windows and inside, the glow of the sacred fire could be seen flickering about. People were withdrawing, their heads covered, in reverence to the goddess within. Then the bath foundations rose high from their marshy origins, the hot water serving them channelled from the sacred spring by the Roman engineers. A covered roof held the bathing pool inside and the whole building was supported on pillars and strong walls of stone.

Falerius turned and expected to find Helvius behind him. Instead Attius was there. 'Where is the magistrate, son?' he asked. Attius' keen eyes made him out to be at least fifty paces behind and talking to Tancorix. The slave was on the ground and unpacking a leather satchel from the pack pony, which he handed to his master. Helvius took it and in slinging it over his shoulders rode towards the pair of them avoiding the carriages and the litters of the rich as he went.

'I've got a little business to see to, Falerius. Tancorix will attend to your every need and he has all the money that will be required for your stay. We will meet up again tonight or a little earlier if I can get away. My apologies and I trust that you understand. Until later then!' and he was gone, lost in the crowded street. Falerius felt abandoned amongst the hordes like he had done as a soldier watching the cowardly run away when under attack and not standing their ground. However an enormous smile erupted when Tancorix let on that his master had gone to solicit the kind of sex that he couldn't get at home. 'As he's ridden for two days I bet that his cock is too sore to perform,' Tancorix dared to say. 'His wife never travels with him. She has her favourite in the household,' he added. Hearing that made Falerius think of Longinus who hadn't crossed his mind until then. He was getting to know what being away on business meant to the respectable magistrate and Falerius unable to catch him in the act personally, wasn't to benefit from his deceptions through bribery.

Tancorix suggested that the animals be stabled and then he could arrange accommodation for the three of them. He wasn't too certain himself that Helvius would be joining them that evening yet was confident of his own instructions. With this many people in the town at once it was important to find a bed, which he did, whilst Falerius and his son dined simply on a lunch of fish and pork lightly cooked over a griddle bar. The afternoon sun continued in its relentless course across the heavens and beat down upon the heads of the pilgrims still drifting by in their one's and two's. The dark skinned Tancorix returned and with his nimble agility easily led the pair through the streets and to their room, where Falerius collapsed onto the bed listening to the noise of the street below through partially closed, though not sleeping orange eyes. Attius was leaning out of the window and pointing at things his father couldn't see.

'We'll go soon, son. I just need a little rest after the ride and lunch,' he said his mind turning to Helvius. Falerius felt truly envious of the magistrate who at that very moment was probably having his bronzed skin oiled whilst pushing his face into the young girl's breasts. Another would be sucking at his loins in an attempt to find a response. No vice or pleasure would evade Helvius that day and, after all, he could afford it. Falerius felt the need to stir himself, and rolled off the bed to stand up. 'The baths are available,' said Tancorix having knocked at the door and standing in the frame. 'I have arranged a private room for you Falerius, and a swim for your little boy,' although Attius wasn't quite that little any more. It was an ideal end to the day for Falerius and what they had come to do; bathe in the waters of Minerva. He wasn't keen on any pre bathing exercises with ball or sticks. He wanted to relax and he wanted to forget. This had been Helvius' idea, he was paying for it and in some way it was going towards repairing the damage the man had caused. Tancorix, skilfully mixing Latin and his native Celtic tongue, opened the doors closed to others and through them Falerius could hear the sounds of the bath. There was splashing as people dived and jumped in. A musician played a doleful tune that fitted its stone surrounding reverberating amongst the shouting and occasionally becoming lost before resurfacing again at a higher pitch. Then Falerius saw the great pool for the first time, resplendent in its man made setting, the green waters looking stagnant and still without flow. In his mind he hadn't been certain of what to expect. The normal course of bathing was to get hot in a steam room and then plunge oneself into the icy waters of a cold pool. It was different here and the noise trapped by the roof prevented it from escaping to the skies above along with the steam. The warm mist gently rose from the surface of the water and filled his nostrils with an air of excitement. He may never again return and so Falerius was determined to make the most of it.

Attius was willingly taken off by one of the attendants and under supervision would be allowed to swim in the pool, whilst Falerius was led into an ante room with bright painted walls depicting sea creatures and their guardian Neptune. The reds, blues and yellows were masterly and in the middle of the room stood a couch. Around the edge were occasional bronze legged tables and a stone bust of Minerva herself. Incense burned quietly in a shallow dish and the disruptive noise of the baths quelled by the closing of the stout wooden door through which he had come. Tancorix spoke quietly to another slave whilst Falerius wandered about the room marvelling at the craftsmanship of the painting, and then he left, leaving Falerius and the slave alone. The slave gestured to Falerius to undress and he lay on the couch with a towel to cover him. Then, in moving closer the slave poured perfumed oil from a small glass pot onto his skin and with strong skilful fingers began to work it in. He repeated the application before turning Falerius over and easing the muscles in his forearms, legs and chest. His shoulders were last, after which the slave scooped the excess off with a strigil. Falerius gazed at the flat wooden rafters and roof above him. He was relaxed and far from home. Far from Julia and their troubles.

Tancorix crept through the wooden door briefly allowing the noise to return before silencing it again. In his hand he carried a small jug of wine and a plate of fresh mussels. 'My master wishes that you want for nothing,' he said before placing the offering down on a table. 'Please . . .' and he poured a cup of wine out for Falerius to drink. The liquid was ruby red, spicy to the nose, strong and unwatered. Through the clear thin glass walls of the jug Bacchus called and Falerius helped himself to another cup savouring the richness of its taste. 'Is my son behaving himself?' he asked sitting up on the side of the couch rubbing a bead of sweat from his brow with his hand. His head tumbled in thought and his speech slow in delivery. The answer was yes and they had found somebody willing enough to take the lad around the whole site and answer his boundless questions. 'Would Falerius like to try the waters himself?' Tancorix suggested and a tired body slowly walked down the steps into the green enveloping warmth of the great pool itself. Falerius sank below the waters and felt the tiredness release its grip on his body. He watched as the sunlight idly moved across the open carved stone windows high above, casting its shadows as it went. The afternoon was drawing on and would the bath shut? Tancorix had reassured him that as it was light then they would stay open longer and if necessary people shown out by the light of oil lamps!

When ready, Falerius was to return to the ante room, which he obediently did to be dried off, oiled and massaged for a second time. Nothing was of any consequence for him as he lay there; he felt free and unburdened of his own life. Every disappointment up to now was being skilfully swept away by the strong fingers of the slave looming large above him and swaying to and fro as he went about his profession. Falerius was soon drifting into idle sleep and recalling the day that he was once woken by a slave summoning him to hear that he was being discharged from the army. Never again did he want to wake to such bad news.

'Falerius pardon me,' Tancorix quietly said, 'I have overspent our money although my master did say to spoil you.'

'What?' a groggy Falerius replied, trying to wake from his dreaming. He didn't understand what Tancorix wanted. 'You require some money, is that it?' he offered.

'No. I was to ask you to sign for me to extend my credit as I cannot find Helvius,' Tancorix added, parchment and pen at the ready. 'One moment,' Falerius said and he stood up. His back was warm from having been lying on it and his whole body tingled from its massage. In the cooling air of the room he suddenly looked and felt older. 'Show me.'

Tancorix pointed at a row of figures and underneath Falerius could make out through reddened eyes the blurred name of Gaius Helvius Bonus. 'There please,' the slave said.

'It is costing me nothing,' smiled Falerius as he duly signed where indicated and passed the pen back to Tancorix. The parchment was carefully rolled up into a leather tube and the top closed. Tancorix and the letter then disappeared leaving Falerius to pour himself another cup of wine. Having drunk it and not really enjoying its taste any more, he returned to the cooling couch and his fitful dreaming where he eventually fell asleep.

CHAPTER VII

STORMS

In the presence of Falerius, Julia tried her hardest not to laugh. She wasn't mocking him but relishing in detail what Attius was telling her. Falerius: drunk? No. Naked: No. Asleep: Certainly not! This wasn't any description of the man that she had known all her adult life. Yet there he was, Attius, telling his mother his innocent tale of their visit to the baths with carefree abandon.

Attius' tour of the baths and the sacred spring from where the mysterious waters issued above ground had ended when the guide returned him to the main building. Their attendants were busying themselves by locking up whilst other slaves cleaned about making ready for the next day. Voices echoed in the empty spaces of many dark corners. Nobody had remembered seeing the boy's father coming in and it was only via a room to room search that he was located at all. As the lock turned and the solid door pushed wide open Attius was suddenly embarrassed to have to witness his father slumped on the couch fast asleep. The room now cold stunk of stale air, old incense and cheap perfumed oils which only hours before had been regarded as his luxury. On the side table Attius saw the empty wine flask and could very quickly see that his father had been drinking. Falerius was helped to his feet by the attendants who also obligingly found his clothes for him and urged him to get dressed. Attius clearly remembered it being late as he could see the constellations through the windows of the great pool room as they were leaving. Then after being ejected they found their way back to their room, went without food for the night and endured another poor sleep. Falerius was angry at himself for neither Helvius nor Tancorix were anywhere to be found. He knew it unwise to have made the journey but couldn't quite accept why. What had gone wrong and why was his trust being so poorly given?

When both men eventually turned up the next morning demanding that they all leave soon, Falerius' suspicions grew wildly. They, by their demeanour had had a good night's rest and were the fresher for the ride home. So much so that the dust on the surface could have been blown away by the speed of their travelling with their fellow travellers pushed aside. Falerius recalled Helvius being far quieter than he had been on the way there although not as friendly. He almost appeared to shun him and resent his company. Nothing was said about it but Falerius wanted to chide him for having the strength to ride a horse so fast when all he had done was ride a whore the night before. He chased him for his answers whilst Attius and Tancorix raced behind.

'Answers?' Julia asked still listening to the tale before her. 'Attius. That's enough, leave us please. What answers?' she again asked.

'I don't know,' stumbled Falerius and struggling with the truth. 'I think that I may have signed a loan agreement. There were figures and the magistrate's name upon a page yet Tancorix had plenty of money!'

'Money for what?' asked the woman who had never had any money lavished upon her or had not been spoilt in any way. The idea of wasting money upon simple pleasures was unheard of and completely obscene. 'And what pleasure was there, Falerius?' she accusingly put to him. 'What did you find so pleasurable apart from the bottom of your cup!' Falerius hid his smile for fear of repercussion. Helvius had received more than a good rub down whilst he had been locked in a cold room alone. 'He must be laughing about his fields and tables at me,' he said. 'Has Cornix been around?' The subject changed.

'No'

'And has Longinus looked after you?' he had to ask.

'Yes,' she replied. 'He has been loyal and true.'

Falerius needed to escape and left the room to think. Finding a comfortable hiding place he pondered the events as they were unfurling. If he had signed something then he could deny it and claim a forgery. Anyway it would require Cominius to sign it too if the loan were to be recognised or called in. He couldn't borrow against what he didn't entirely own and Helvius must know that? What was he going to do? Trick Cominius in the same way that he had apparently been tricked into signing something if indeed it were a trick. It wasn't worth the worry Falerius vowed as his friend would be now far into the proposed military advance to Siluria and out of reach. What was Helvius planning to do? Wait the four months and then upon his return introduce himself as a paunchy, lecherous thief?

In the near distance the sky had grown a menacing grey colour, full of the heat from the previous week and bubbling with restlessness. It rose slowly over the nearest of the trees and filled Falerius' view out to the west. Large drops of rain began to fall and then stopped just as suddenly whilst the wind teased Falerius, first by its stillness and then by its fury. More rain rapidly began to fall and thunder fell across the land like a thousand war horns. High above the rampant darkness a blue haze shone lit by the last of the day's sunlight through which mighty Jupiter could see, as he vent his anger upon humanity below. His lightning bolts dropped to the ground from the boiling skies. Falerius knew it best to shelter from the storm and went back inside. All that evening and all that night the storms drove in upon the chariot wheels of the furious gods and, long after the swinging oil lamps had been extinguished, they continued playing with the fears of the mortal beings cowering in their hovels and their villas far below.

The morning brought with it the sound of rain dripping from the roof and low mists began to form following cold rain lying on the warm earth. A chill filled the air and one in which Falerius could be found working hard to keep his damp spirits up. He stood upon the roof of the house and arched his back for comfort having been busy hammering home another nail into the tile locating it into the black empty hole from where it had come. Around him there were other black holes urgently requiring his attention. The house was an island in a sea of mud and puddles and, as Falerius looked out over his fields, he could see more damage inflicted by the storms. Trees, blown over, rested helplessly on their sides, their limbs propping them up for support, their roots torn from the earth. Rutted farm tracks were filled with water and flowed like a thousand rivers from the same source. Falerius went back to his hammering which was proving a welcome distraction from Julia's incessant desire to know more about his visit to Aquae Sulis. She wanted to ask more and more as to his dealings, yet what about her and Longinus? He couldn't prove anything. When was it all going to end and where?

A day after the storm Cornix unexpectedly arrived with the workmen promised by Helvius and they were soon put to work by an eager Falerius. In their cart they had brought along spades, shovels, picks and axes to both speed up the repair work and get the farm cleared of debris. Ditches were cleared so that the water drained from the fields although it soon pooled up again further down stream where rubbish had been washed into the channel. Falerius' sheep stood motionless on the mounds of dry ground that were available to them and watched whilst the spring beneath the hill, recharged with energy, forced a copious supply of icy cold water out. In the group of men, none were familiar to Falerius by sight and that pleased him enormously for he couldn't cope with the sniggering behind his back. Cornix didn't stay long either explaining that he had another estate to administer to and would be away for up to a couple of months and the men were to be under Falerius' command until Helvius, requiring them himself, called them back. True to his word, he had also included in the group a tutor who being a little put out at having to travel and mix with such company as this, arrived full of complaints. He thought himself worthy of better and asked to meet his pupil. Attius was duly summoned and the unlikely partnership put to the test in the only place where it was going to be quiet – the barn. More complaining followed in the guise of it being unsuitable for learning and oratory. How could the boy regard himself as being educated from sitting on hay and dirt? Julia, the diplomat solved the problem with a little cloth and food.

'We took Alexandria!' the tutor boomed referring to Rome's early military glories and then went on to explain further about the empire by drawing a rough map in the dirt. 'This will never do boy. How can you expect to learn anything from the earth?' he said fussing with his toga and quietly expressing a delight that somebody else was paying for him to be there. 'I don't know how much I can teach you in a day,' he added unsure of whether or not he would be coming back. 'I suppose we could do some arithmetic! How are you at your sums?' Attius looked at him and wondered if with all the dithering he would ever learn anything worth knowing.

'Is the empire only full of Celts and Romans fighting each other?' he asked the tutor hoping to be expelled for his troubles and thus be freed to go and ride Roma.

'How little you know!' his teacher replied walking off and mumbling to himself. He accepted that he would have to come back regularly if Attius was to have any kind of education at all, but nobody had said for how long or who was going to pay for it all. Certainly Falerius had not the money to school his son and Helvius had given no indication of his intentions in the matter. It was like planting a vine, nurturing it weekly throughout its growth and then expecting it to yield a fine vintage. It wasn't going to be possible. Attius however, free of the rigidity of learning, made the most of his spare time and as a boy growing quickly required the physical demands of outside work and play thrust upon him by his father. The city, as the tutor had told him, was destined to last twelve hundred years and Attius was keen to play his part in this destiny for all Romans. Riding across the wide open hills helped him dream of the endless patrols required by the empire to keep its borders safe from invasions, with the glorious chapters of Britannia written by poets and recited safely, far away in the finest houses of Rome. There would be no creature on earth that didn't eventually bow down to its glory!

Attius had come to notice that the camp fire stories so beloved by his father were coming to an end now with the arrival of the teacher. He recalled the tales of five hundred legionaries desperately struggling to prevent the sacred eagle from being captured on the field of battle by savages so driven to war that they would attack with all thoughts for their own safety abandoned. Their wild, slashing sword blows, difficult to defend with cumbersome shields left men falling to the ground clutching at the most grotesque of wounds to head and leg. Gone too were the stories of men huddled together at night for protection, frightened of lighting a fire lest it gave them away and fearfully listening to the vast array of strange sounds forever coming closer. Falerius it seemed didn't care for the army and was taking on, more and more, the stoicism of the farmer. Attius had noticed him becoming quieter, introverted yet not at all cautious. He gambled on his arguments with Julia and was developing an unshakable confidence in the future. Little by little, Gaius Helvius Bonus was saving him, building him up. The house, now repaired, looked better and the ditches, free of their obstructions, allowed the passage of water thus aiding the drainage of the fields. Small reserves of clay had been dug out ready for the next shearing and the farm tracks made passable again by repairs of good river gravel sourced locally. All Falerius had to do was dance to his patron's tune and this he was learning to do. Why had he doubted the man? The system was there and all Falerius had to do was accept his part in it, at the bottom. Helvius would continue throwing invitations out as and when they were needed to reward his clients for their support and supplication, and Falerius would gratefully accept a free meal. Julia tried to warn him of this developing friendship bought with gifts but to Falerius it was a necessary part of business and he was beginning to understand his role in it all the better. He would have none of her doubts and was unable to see the stamp of the magistrate upon his very land in the imprint of a worker's hobnailed sole.

The quiet 'treaty' that existed between the soldier and the magistrate continued well into the autumn of that year with Julia being left to remind Falerius that Cominius' tour of duty ought to be over and he could be expecting him soon. The fields, naked of their harvest couldn't support an army on patrol and soon they would have to return to their forts for the season. It was normal military practice and Falerius knew it.

Only in exceptional circumstances would a war be prosecuted into the harsh months of winter with all its problems of supply and communication. Falerius knew of no reason for his friend to be away as idle market gossip locally hadn't mentioned any troubles in the west and Cominius himself had stated how well protected they were to be. At this very moment the engineer soldier would be packing away his groma for another year and readying himself for a visit. Only the slow onset of winter skies from the north and the drifting snowflakes in the wind could deter Falerius from thinking otherwise. His friend would return to see Helvius buying his wool. The once vulnerable Falerius was now safe and could again sit before the fire at night making plans for his son to eventually take over the farm.

Only Cominius never arrived. Nor his slave Marcus and the old year was at its turn. Saturn was to die and Saturn was to be reborn again. To celebrate this most noble of December feasts, Saturnalia, Helvius had invited his clients and their families to his home where green, red and blue candles would be lit, games played and presents given. The master would become the slave and vice versa which was to suit Falerius as he only had the one. Helvius was to choose his bailiff Cornix, safely back from wherever he had been, to be Master of the Revels. He would dress as the magistrate and Helvius would dress as the slave and the two men act accordingly for the duration of the holiday. Accommodation would be provided for the familes so that they would not have to endure the perils of travelling through a winter's night. Attius' excitement grew at the prospect of a party for he had no reason to dislike the magistrate and indeed needed to thank him personally for supplying his tutor. Julia, without reason for celebration agreed to attend for she disliked the fuss of religion, and Falerius once again in stoical mood, wished his friend were to be there.

With the frost veneered to the dark folds in the hillside and with Sol unable to peel it back due to his lowly stature in the winter sky, festivities began. The smell of roasting meats met Falerius as he entered Helvius' villa retreat, with the greetings brief and curt as more of the magistrates' clients were being entertained the same day. It was a seasonal 'thank you' that guaranteed Helvius their voting support; for without it he would be unable to continue in his civic duty of caring for them. In the old soldier's eyes it was wanton gluttony and a situation difficult to accept. How could the master and slave exchange places? A soldier always respected his superior officer even if he regarded him as a fool and there was a natural order to things reinforced at times by harsh discipline. Cornix, today back from his travels had now found himself elevated to Master of the Revels and placed at the head of the top table. Falerius along with his family had been shown to the lower table and the one closest to the busy smoking kitchen.

Helvius, today's slave and fool came forward with a first course of lentils and chestnuts at which one of his guests cried out 'You've skimped on the honey, cheapskate! What am I to do? Suck my fingers for flavouring!' Helvius laughed at having to endure their mocking for the one day. In a week's time he would be master again and have plenty of reason to remember their jibes, however innocently given. The next course of lamb cooked with ginger was presented to the guests and their baiting was that in not being able to taste Helvius' spices, they wished that they had brought along their own to flavour the bland, slightly off food. A small red faced man next to Falerius seemed to be goading his host admirably and the warmth of the room plus the extravagant wines provided by Helvius made his features appear to be as bright as the candle that flickered at his side. Falerius too felt the warmth, wiping sweat off his forehead. This was a far cry from the formal party that he had attended previously and, from the vantage point of his lowly table he winced at the revelry before him. Attius was enjoying himself watching people disregard their social status in the name of celebrating the death and rebirth of Saturn. Religion could be fun and nearly everybody was full of wine except for his father, Helvius and Cornix. With the smell of cumin heavy in the smoky air and a dish of honey glazed ham and oysters before him

Attius returned to thinking of his own stomach. Food such as this wasn't served in his home. Helvius, stained from the kitchen, continued to bring in the beets, parsnips and carrots to add to the meal parrying the insults as he went.

When at last the final course of honey fried dates and smoked cheese appeared Falerius found that he could relax a little. The red faced man lying next to him had succumbed to drowsiness and was close to sleep whilst the rancour that had filled the room had died away to a quiet chatter amongst friends. The storm that was chaos before him had died down dulled by food and an excess of drink sufficient to overwhelm the hardiest of diners. Only a few drowsy eyes remained open to witness Helvius, who was wearing an ill fitting stained slave's tunic hanging below his knees prompt Cornix into giving the customary presents. A hand clapped somewhere and then silence fell. 'Cornix!' the magistrate urged and his bailiff rose idly to his feet. He was dressed in all the finery of the toga, wearing gold rings upon his fingers and the best food on his plate, yet in his mouth sat the cruellest of words.

'Guests, welcome!' he meekly said. 'I hope that all have dined sufficiently for the gods to have heard you and now it is time for me to deliver one present to a friend amongst us.' He stopped talking and only the glare of his master's eyes could have forced him to continue. In them he saw the menace that he had seen often before.

'Come, Cornix. You are Master of the Revels, a noble role. Do not be shy before us and betray my trust in you!' Helvius spoke.

All eyes watched him turn for Falerius. The old soldier had been toying with his meal and looking forward to resting his bloated stomach in bed. He had asked for and been offered some pickled lettuce in an attempt to settle his food. He had felt uncomfortable all evening long and was careful at eating anything else in case it was the cause of his immediate discomfort. He felt warm and clammy and on a night where the cold outside was sucking the living warmth from the very earth, freezing all that was stationary into silver statues of frost. Cornix moved closer.

'Falerius . . . there is this to give you,' he said at which Falerius looked up in surprise at his outstretched hand. Cornix allowed the lead fob to fall into his grip and backed away. 'I'm sorry for your loss,' he said. Out of the corner of his eye Falerius could see Helvius intently staring at him.

'What is it?' he said rolling it between his fingers and reading quietly to himself what was inscribed on the warm soft lead. There were just the three words:

JULIUS COMINIUS CIVILIS

'Where did you get this?' he asked.

'Your friend is dead.'

'Dead? What do you mean?'

'Falerius, you have to believe that we received news of a soldier in Corinium showing signs of plague. It was Cominius. He was seriously ill with fever, sweating and delirium. The doctor said that he must be isolated and that his chances of living were poor,' Cornix explained.

Helvius took his chance and butted in 'For the public good, Falerius, for the public good. We couldn't risk others catching it.'

'What public good?' Falerius shouted waking the dead drunk around him. 'Why did nobody summon me?'

Cornix went on 'It was only when he was close to death that we could make out where he had been travelling and realised that he was a friend of yours. The fever eventually took him although we prayed long into the night that the gods spare him. Death then devoured him and took him away. It was his destiny. You will appreciate also that the magistrate had to act quickly and dispose of the body to prevent any spreading of the disease. They ordered that his body be cremated immediately and that this tag be given to you. We did our best for your friend, Falerius, and have given him the due rites.'

'Where was his slave, Marcus? Was he there?'

'No, Falerius. There was no sign of him. You as an ex-soldier will appreciate the dangers that arise from fresh troop reinforcements from abroad. They bring with them disease and that is what Cominius had caught.' Cornix's simple explanation didn't sound entirely convincing in its delivery of how his friend had come to die.

The room of fools had fallen silent whilst Julia put her arms around Falerius' shoulders allowing him to cry gently for his friend. Attius said sorry and without having seen it, he had thought the tag in his father's hand was similar to one that he had plucked from the river bed earlier in the year. It wasn't and so he kept quiet.

'Cornix has another present, Falerius. Would you like to see it?' Helvius, the soft fat slave of the evening looking ridiculous in his garb and smoke stained face beckoned the Master of the Revels to step forward and deliver more bad news. Cornix approached clutching a leather tube inside which he tapped out a piece of parchment, holding it between his hands to read out aloud. To Falerius it looked similar to the one that Tancorix had with him in Aquae Sulis before he disappeared. Helvius then moved in taking the parchment from Cornix' hands and wanting to read it himself. 'I quote,' he said loudly, 'that you Falerius':

Have agreed to sign over all deeds and rights to White Horse villa estate to Gaius Helvius Bonus for his protection and discretion. No claim can be made against this deed and your son forfeits all claims to his inherited rights to your property

And there was Falerius' name and signature.

Falerius laughed out aloud. 'That can't be right. I have never signed an agreement like that before. You are out to trick me!' His back was now against the wall and Cominius his ally was dead.

'It's a legal document, Falerius.' Helvius said now reassuming the master's role and moving in for the kill. 'You can of course continue farming there for me but in the absence of your friend's will you have no recourse to what you have signed. The farm is mine. You have struggled with what the good earth has given you and now I will make it pay! Of course you are free to appeal and we will hear your case. Then of course, Falerius if you are not satisfied you can always take your case to the Emperor or the Governor himself wherever they happen to be!'

The room erupted into murmurs of discontent, for all present there had been cheated by Helvius at one time or another, but not to this extent. Falerius was an ex soldier and that stood for something in their eyes although they knew to their individual cost that Helvius was a bully and a coward too and that he would protect himself above all others. Yet the murmuring remained just that. Cornix took the parchment back and carefully replaced it in its seal at which Falerius leapt from his couch scattering the dishes of uneaten food as he went. He lunged at Helvius but two slaves standing by for such a move intervened and held him tight with an intense struggle. The sweat on his brow increasing, his heart thumping but his breath becoming harder to draw, Falerius fought on to the end. He called out for Attius before clawing at his chest in an agonising burst of pain. The room spun around and Falerius fell to the floor dead, lying prostrate over the tiled mosaic face of Aeneas, the legendary founder of Rome.

CHAPTER VIII
FAREWELL FALERIUS

I am Ulpius, a friend of Julianus Falerius Silvanus, and I too, witnessed his death. For speaking out like this I expect my farm to be raided in the late hours of the night by cowards who will destroy my hay crop in the barn and release my animals to the perils of the woods. No sanctuary will be offered by these creatures and none expected by me. It will be convenient for them to lose their memories and shrink away from the deeds of Gaius Helvius Bonus. Those who call Falerius' death both accidental and unfortunate are not men in my eyes. However that didn't stop many from crying out aloud that evening in their desperate attempts at reassuring the dead man's spirit that it would be sorely missed. The superstitious idiots! Only the living can exact any kind of revenge and the true merits of that revenge can then be discussed at leisure in the afterlife.

How Julia cried for him long into the night and how tenderly she closed his eyes. The strength of her life cut away and the boy Attius could only stare in hatred at Helvius and his Saturnalian fool Cornix. What presents had they given him? The boy in tears, I remember, getting up to confront those who had conspired to kill his father. The shouting coming from his mouth uselessly bleeding into the wailing of his friends until he could cry no more. His heart drained of its feelings was rapidly turning to stone.

I remember Helvius wanting to throw a cloak of authority over the affair and in doing so gain the best of reputations for himself through offering unsolicited support for the defenceless Julia. Out of some kind of decency the body of Falerius was taken to another room and washed before being wrapped in a woollen shroud. The magistrate, used to being in control, guided the innocent hand of Attius throughout the ordeal and promised to take care of the funeral. With chosen words he dismissed the petitions of those who may not have been so drunk as to have witnessed the drama and with others chosen coins did the trick in securing their silence. Attius may not have been totally aware of all the implications but Julia soon was. As rightful heir to his father's property he would only receive his personal possessions, as the land and the farm were now in the ownership of Gaius Helvius Bonus and like the magistrate had said, the boy could appeal to the other magistrate if he so wished. I would be prepared to speak up at any investigation but who would be brave enough to risk an approach to the Governor; and Julia, who was going to take care of her? In a quiet private conversation between the two, Julia and Bonus, I remember her telling me, that in triumphant victory tones falling from the magistrate's mouth he 'would be seeing to her' in the same way as he would be 'seeing to her son.' She well understood the implications and after all, who else was there for her? Attius would have to fend for himself the best he could, and she hated herself for thinking that. Unbeknown, Bonus had plans for the boy and those plans excluded his mother. Julia also went on to describe in lurid detail how the old man had run his finger along her nose, across her lips and down across her chin. 'Excellent,' he moaned as his fingers ran further across her breast-bone and then settled on pushing her clothing to one side feeling her breast. 'Your soldier had everything to fight for and now you mourn his passing. You know that I will take care of you and that you can stay in the farmhouse. Your son however will be leaving.' He wouldn't elaborate any further.

'My son! What are you going to do?' she hissed.

'The army: that is where he is going. Hasn't he wanted to all this time?'

Again true to his word Helvius paid for the funeral although the profits would be coming from the estate of Falerius. The procession was to leave from his villa and solemnly follow the shortest path to Julia's home, although the body of Falerius was to be carried most of the way on a cart. A pyre had been arranged and both mourners and musicians assembled in due ceremonial order. The day was bright, cold and crisp and good for seeing the dead off as the priest remarked referring to the fact that the

116

body would burn quickly and cleanly. Every step along the way a dirge would sound from the horn and bounce off the iron-hard hillside to the south, returning a short time later as if to remind everyone of their purpose. Life could be short and the journey hereafter much longer if the due reverences were not paid heed to, and nobody, especially Helvius Bonus, wanted the unhappy spirit of Falerius to return and haunt him.

Julia walked alongside Attius. Their sad conversation was quiet and hushed.

At the end of their living journey the bearers lifted Falerius' corpse onto the pyre, which was then lit. Everybody stood silently; their heads covered out of respect and their faces watching the smoke rise into a blue sky. Falerius had gone and once cooled, the ashes were collected and ritually washed in wine to purify them. They were then carefully placed into a clay pot for Julia to hold. The hole to receive them in the earth was dug and Helvius, speaking a few words about the dead man's life, announced that the tombstone would be erected when completed which would be soon. Julia walked towards the empty ground. In her hands she held the charred remains of the man that she had loved. As the cold of the winter's day bit a little more she didn't want to risk dropping the casket and so avoided drawing her clothes tighter about her until handing it to Attius who was already kneeling. Once safely in his grasp she stood up straight and pulled the warmth in from her cloak. She looked down. Attius lowered his father's remains to the flat bottom of the hole and pulled a little of the dark earth over them.

'Mother, he will need to eat . . .' He said at which sign Julia beckoned a friend to pass her another pot full of food scraps for the long journey through the Underworld. The pot was heavier than Attius had anticipated and with cold hands, he nearly dropped it, spilling and revealing its precious contents. There had been enough food in there to sink Charon's boat he later joked with her. The hole was reverently filled in and Falerius gone from the world that they knew, though all stayed a while afterwards to feast with his spirit.

Julia was now keen for the day to end. It had been a hard walk from Helvius' villa, the day bitterly cold and full of emotion. She knew what the future was to bring for her but was still unsure as to that of her son. The magistrate had not overlooked this and as the small group of friends and mourners dispersed he revealed his plans.

'Tomorrow you are to leave for Isca. I have prepared an introductory letter for you to hand into the recruiting officer and you are to take that slave of yours, your horse and go and never return. I have recommended the cavalry and may they send you far away where their need is the greatest – the far north! If you do return there will be nothing here for you. I am your friend and doing this in your interest. This farm will become a larger estate and your house a home for slaves.' He handed over the letter to Attius who despised the earth he stood upon. 'I will be back tomorrow to speak with your mother,' he said and left.

Attius and Julia spent their last night beside a brazier that Longinus had lit for them discussing their future. The room was warm and the night sky outside revolved silently in its motion devoid of ghosts or visions. Julia felt Falerius close by and burst into tears at the thought of her son being so far away. They embraced tightly and Attius vowed his return. He would save every coin given to him by the army, win even more in dangerous combat and take all that could be his for the taking. He was now a man but could his mother be strong enough to wait for his return or would Bonus drive her to her death as he had Falerius? It seemed so senseless thinking of it all as the future was untold. Instead he spent the remaining few hours that they had together talking of the past. It had been a hard life that had brought them to where they were now and in a way Attius was keen to make his own mark upon the world. The hazel spear of long ago and the riding forays over the hills were just memories. As a young man he felt nervously ready to win himself a military reputation that his father would have been proud to see.

A crunch on the crystal snow outside heralded the magistrate's early arrival. There was no knock at the door as he let himself in and found all three of them ready for the day ahead. Julia had prepared food for the journey and Longinus had saddled the horses. A brief exchange of words between Attius and Helvius ensued, after which they all went outside into the fresh morning air. The two mounted after which the magistrate, putting his arm around Julia's shoulders ushered her back indoors closing the door behind him. Attius stared at the wooden planks longing to see through them and witness the goings on inside. Everything in an instant suddenly appeared empty – his heart, his life and his future. Around, a fog started to lie on the ground like a shroud and it was into this that he had to turn his horse and begin to leave.

The latch on the main door then suddenly burst open and Attius turned. Across the rutted yard ran his mother clutching a bundle in her arms, which she thrust into the surprised grasp of her son.

'Your father's sword. May it protect you. Now go!'

'Julia!' Bonus called her back like a man would a dog, and she obeyed.

Attius rode away like she had wished, out of the farm entrance and past Cornix who had been posted there in case of trouble. His uncertain future in the army was about to begin.

CHAPTER IX
PRAISE AND DISCIPLINE

'Yes, Marcus Attius Octavianus,' the enrolling officer spoke slowly, tapping the letter of recommendation against his left palm. 'We shall be accepting you provisionally into the army.'

'Your reference,' he continued 'is excellent. You must have friends in high places. It is a very good one, in fact just too good. You are free born? Tell me, where do you come from?'

'To the east of Durocornovium,' Attius meekly replied unsure of the next criticism.

'And you are a sheep farmer's son? Weren't there any other riches to be won from the land?'

'No, sir'

'Tell me, was your father a soldier, too?'

Now free of whatever Helvius Bonus had written upon the wooden pages of his letter the young man enthusiastically answered 'Yes, sir, he was a centurion in Cohort VII Legio Secunda Augusta.' The pride shone through his smile.

'And your father talked of the army did he?'

'Yes. He told me that it was its duty to win land for the Emperor so that others, in his name, may farm in peace. He sometimes also talked about battles that he had fought in . . .'

The enrolling officer dismayed by Attius' simple answer got up from his chair and walked to the open window resting his arm on the ledge and gazed out. He was smartly dressed in a white tunic and leggings with a warm cloak thrown over his shoulder. Across his waist ran a carefully engraved belt from which hung his small dagger, the pugio. The room was warm considering the time of year and slowly being darkened by the falling afternoon sun. His mind was full of hostile talk of wanting to fight bravely, draw the sword on a hundred enemies and return from battle with all the booty that could be won. Not one recruit that short day had mentioned their fellow soldiers. That was all the ammunition that he needed and returning to Attius he attacked again.

'Listen to me,' he said. 'You are joining the army to ride in its cavalry whilst our divine Caesar Hadrianus has asked for peace and no more expansion. We are to obey here, as they are to obey in Germania, Dacia and Africa. Do you understand?'

Attius, remembering the schooling that Bonus had provided years before, was confident of knowing where those places were. 'My father said . . .'

'STOP!' shouted the officer causing his clerk to look up from the wooden desk. 'Did your father die a glorious death defending the legionary eagle or was he lost on a far frontier?' He fiddled with his dagger whilst waving his right arm about in the foul air. 'Have your family a famous victor in their shrine to the Lares, Attius, or did he die in his bed. Come tell me, for you have an excellent reference.'

'No sir.'

'Then exactly where did he die Attius?'

Unashamed, Attius replied that he had died at a dinner party.

There followed a short period of silence that almost served to respect the spirit of Falerius after which the enrolment continued.

'You have requested to join an Ala. That will come in time but first you must learn about the army and its ways. You may find yourself in a warm land where the natives are easily bribed and never have to throw your spear in anger, or you may serve here in the wet and cold forever watching over a far off hillside for signs of a massing army. You must go where you are sent and on occasions you must shear those farmers too for their taxes. Without expansion there is to be no more money so we must ensure that everybody is paying the procurator their share. Unfortunately peace won't pay for itself.'

Attius was keen to ask if there was the opportunity under this regime to have more money for himself above his army salary. Could he be promoted?

'Attius, without war there is no death. Without death there is no promotion and you may have to watch somebody die at their dining couch,' he sarcastically added. 'Now go. My clerk has allocated you this barrack block. Your training begins tomorrow and I am confident that you are fit enough to serve. If after four months you are seen as unsuitable then we will dismiss you,' he said adding 'Also you are not to buy land whilst serving the army.'

Attius turned and opened the heavy wooden door that led out into the courtyard of the Principium. Everyone framed there was a stranger to him from the Legate's limping groom to the sentry walking at a snail's pace high upon the rampart wall. He missed his mother and could not understand what his own father had seen in serving as soldier in the name of Rome. As a boy Attius had always lived beyond the reach of the walls at risk of being cast out to danger at a moment's notice if they were ever assaulted. Their shadows had no substance of protection in them and now as a young man he felt trapped by them yearning again to be free. Back inside the office the recruiting officer instructed his clerk to put a sign against Attius' name. 'He asks too many questions,' he said watching him make his mark in black sooty ink. A splash of sand confirmed his order by drying the ink; the page was then rolled up and a record kept to be sent to the army offices in Italia if Attius ever passed his probationary period four months hence.

Lying on his bunk that evening and listening although not concentrating too deeply on what exactly was being said, Attius put his time instead to thought. What was it that had brought him here? Outside the walls his closest ally Longinus, the slave, had found a bed for the night too. He would have to adapt to the new order and find himself work possibly in the bath house or in the fields for someone else. Attius' postings weren't certain and it would be a long time before he could silently buy land of his own on his salary and get Longinus to farm it as a proxy thus avoiding the army rules. Roma, the trusted pony of old, had been sold to raise money along with the farm's other beast, and with this limited supply Attius could keep Longinus on a little longer. He thought now that he had become the slave instead; only a slave to the army, to go where he was sent and to do what he was told. Those benefits that his small shared room of colleagues spoke of were to mean little – the training, the regular food, the pay and the adventure. Attius' thoughts turned to his mother and again the overwhelming sense of hopelessness devoured him like death devouring life. This was his destiny and he thought about the lead curse tablet he chose from the river crossing that warm summer's day. At his age he wasn't the youngest and, having had the chance to physically compare them, neither was he the weakest. There was little fear at what was to come and Attius openly welcomed the immediate future, if only as a diversion from those nagging thoughts that this hadn't entirely been his choice. He might have enlisted, but in his time and not Gaius Helvius Bonus'. He vowed silently to win awards that could lead to money and glory. Outside in the massing dark of the mountains there must still be insurrection brewing amongst the tribes. There had to be just a flicker of resistance remaining ready to blow into another firestorm, or were they so utterly beaten and cowed as to accept their lot? Attius the soldier simply couldn't believe in peace as it served no purpose to an army.

The room of recruits began to settle down for the night and their potential twenty five years, with or without the same friends. The youngest if he were to survive could still enjoy the remainder of his life outside the fortress walls and Attius, now trapped by the stark stone barrack room walls, worried for his future. Friendships could be brief and not enduring although all there were expected to share common dangers together and through them strong bonds of loyalty would grow. Where would he serve? It could be a far off deserted frontier posting, devoid of humanity and a long way from his mother. Attius had thought about the chances of seeing her again and dismissed them. The others in that room had forgotten about all traces of home too as a sign of bravado, although they were probably lying. Britannia, although at peace was a drawing ground for troops required elsewhere and nobody could truly expect a long posting unless the entire empire stayed that way. Loyalties and troops making themselves at home in permanent forts were frowned upon except at the present where the situation was to suit that purpose. There was to be no more expansion by military might, not unless Hadrianus thought the need serious enough or he was to die and his successor reversed that policy.

What of the immediate threats though: The bullying, the bribes or the boredom that can come from military service. The legalities began to bother him; no marrying the local girls meant that relationships were not meant to last. Attius thought about his father and mother. What was it that had brought them together and kept them together in a world where the rules were for men only? Everything about him seemed so remote from that day when he chose his hazel spear and yearned for a fight with Longinus the Celt, his natural enemy.

There were six recruits in Attius' room and a few empty bunks. The army weren't naturally conscripting because losses were few in peace-time and the seven had arrived via volunteering, the prefered way to gain new soldiers as they fought better. His fellow recruits had come by way of a younger brother being recommended because of the inheritance laws for example or just an adventurer seeing where his luck would lead him. All were healthy and fit and Attius looked forward to the challenge of who was to be the best amongst them. Out of the corner of his eye he selected the strongest to befriend and listened in on their idle chat, pick-ing out the words that he himself would have chosen to use and silently laughing at what they chose to laugh at. There were times when he didn't feel any distance from them at all for they all faced the same discipline. However what marked Attius out that evening was that his eyes wouldn't focus in the dimly lit room and he felt nauseous with a headache too. Like bad luck this had always come on unannounced and the only simple remedy was to lie still and be quiet hoping it would pass. If the conversa-tion came his way then he would reply, but other than that he would choose silence. Tomorrow he secretly hoped that he would be feeling better, for he had a physical examination to face and that would decide his future.

Following a small breakfast all were summoned one by one to see the medicus and have their physical strengths assessed. Were their hands and feet strong enough? Were their buttocks firm and their stomachs flat? Were their arms and legs sinewy and capable of hard work? Were their eyes clear and their hearing good? Lastly could they read and write? Could Attius, however, stand up without feeling that he ought to be falling over? His examination was fortunately punctuated by delays caused by the weather, as late January brought with it squalls of cold volleys from the foothills in the near blue distance. The rain arriving in sheets of driven grey, raced across the tiled roofs of the squat fortress and accumulated in puddles upon the paved streets, the door to the examination room being constantly opened and shut as the incumbents sought refuge from the sky. They were ordered back out again at a bark before the door slammed shut. Attius seized his chance and tried to relax allowing his eyes to take in as much of the available light as there was. This he had learnt from experience and would help his dizziness. The kick from Roma, which he was sure, was the root cause of all his discomfort had been five years or more but, little by little, and now as he grew older, the effects were becoming more evident. Some days the sun would be too bright or Attius undertake one task too many and then the problems start. He knew that they would check his eyesight and look into the eyes to ensure that they were clear and without blemish. He had slept well the previous night and washed his face in cold water to ensure his reactions to questioning were rapid and without prolonged delay in their answer. This worked and Attius passed through unnoticed as being with blemish. To the army medics he was fit for duty. Lastly his height was measured and at less than six roman feet tall he wouldn't see service in an ala but instead be destined for the legionary cavalry, a lesser posting. This was not made known to him but would be revealed at his oath-taking ceremony following training.

Attius thanked the officer and went off with the others to draw their clothes from the stores. There were tunics, a cloak, sandals, scarf and leather riding breeches to collect. The sword, chain mail, shield and spear would all follow in due course and deducted from their pay accordingly. He felt slightly cheated by the payment for a sword especially as he had possession of his father's but realised the folly of trying to use a short stabbing sword on the back of a horse. There were moans from the others about having to be deducted monies already and if the army served to unite people then it was often in disharmony. They would all be alright if the relentless rain didn't rot their steel or leather. Attius looked closely at his cloak and the memories of trying to sell a better quality woollen product in the market at Corinium came flooding back. His fingers played with the greasy fibres until he was absolutely sure in himself that on no account would the army have bought his father's wool. It had been too good for them. On the frontier and in a rainstorm Attius tended to agree with them and wrapped the cloak firmly about his shoulders. He longed for his father to have seen him, not the soldier on parade but the raw recruit beginning his journey in life. He longed for Julia too but realised that she could never be by his side again unless the gods willed it and allowed them one more meeting. Attius wanted so much to be the son that his father would have been proud of and in his turn he would never allow the memory of Falerius to fade way. He felt so alone now and vulnerable, not for himself, but for those who had lived their lives or who were presently suffering at the hands of fate. What was to come for him?

Attius took the rare opportunities granted to him whilst serving in his father's old fort to ask of him and relive old memories. Most were fond and loyal and in particular he was guided towards Gaius Macrius Sulla, the one soldier that Falerius had taken a liking to and encouraged. Macrius was in charge of the ballista and Attius would have to wait until the cavalry and infantry undertook a joint exercise before he could befriend him and tell him of his father's fate. Until then he had other questions that needed answering. Firstly had the other recruits, those that came from the land, been questioned about their farms and the mineral potential. Why would they ask that? He had thought the question odd but without undue worry or hesitation had answered it truthfully.

'Maybe it is to save the procurator the trouble of asking, Attius. A census on us all,' a recruit quipped.

'I've heard it said that gold exists in the mountains further west and maybe they are worried that you have the rest at home,' joked another. 'What have you got to hide, Attius?' he went on.

Attius could only think of his health but he wasn't going to reveal that. Instead he changed the subject to plague.

'Has anybody said anything to you all about an illness? I mean a fever brought to Isca Silurum last year by troops passing through. I heard that there's been plague here,' he said. He wasn't too discreet in his asking, and too loud in his enquiries for the likes of one Optio for a swift blow in the ribs from his stick had Attius tumbling and lying face up before an angry mob. There was nothing more fearful to a soldier than rumour – the commander was dead, the eagle lost, a legion destroyed, the gates have fallen, others are running for their lives and so on. Attius unwittingly accepted the beating that was coming his way and learnt to keep his thoughts to himself.

'Now get back to your barracks and keep your mouth shut,' the Optio whispered through his wheat worn teeth. 'There's been no plague here!'

In his bunk Attius once again had the opportunity of thinking upon his military career. It hadn't started well for him despite Helvius' excellent reference. He thought it bad luck to have been overheard asking questions about the now obvious lies that the magistrate had spread at the Saturnalia dinner where his father had collapsed and died. Bad luck though can lead to desertion and Attius' new friends were soon keeping their distance, not wanting to associate themselves with him in case they too were punished with a public beating. Attius thought about deserting the army altogether but who was there to run to and who would take him in? What gifts to which god would it take in order to free him?

The long month of January dragged on and with it came the tedium of drill, more drill and exercise until February dawned a little lighter and full of more promise of actually riding out. The drill so far had been restricted to saddling and unsaddling the horse, and then mounting and dismounting both on the live animal and over a wooden vaulting horse for practice. What they all desperately needed was a change, brought about by an invocation to Fortuna, and Attius played his part in promising temple gifts in return for a favourable future. Soon all were to be rewarded by a practice ride across the foothills surrounding Isca. Without weapons they may have been vulnerable but the ground, now free of its cloak of snow, was soft enough to allow an unshod hoof some bite into it without slipping and the instructors were confident enough that the small party could evade trouble. On the day of this first practice, they all left via the fort's main gate and the roads leading away to ride over the unbroken countryside around. Their purpose was to evaluate their skills at riding over obstacles whether they were rocks, marsh, woods or streams. They were to keep close and to return that evening as one. All rode bareheaded and with socks on under their sandals and with thick greasy cloaks to keep the cold out they set off. The time of year was unfortunate but the exhilaration at being free of the rigid confines of their training up to now carried them all forward. None thought about the tight discipline or regular boredom of mundane tasks. They were left far behind in the trailing hoof prints.

Attius too, in the semi urban landscape surrounding Isca Silurum forgot about his home. New opportunities were coming of operating beyond these structured fields in the flat river plains and there was hope of being posted into the far mountains beyond. The snow-capped mountains of Siluria were calling to him and he was keen to follow the already well trodden paths of victory towards them. He felt alive and a part of the natural world where the forces of nature were to be conquered; those forces welded by Vulcan's mighty forge. Naturally, to survive he would have to learn to swim the deepest rivers if necessary and build the strongest defences if ever caught away from safety. Hunting skills too would play their part in the quest for mastery over this hostile barren land.

The day's ride eventually ended back at the fort as a blue grey mist pulled the shadows towards darkness and men busied themselves by finding an evening's occupation somewhere. A long single trumpet call sounded the watch over a landscape at peace with itself, whilst the mighty fortress sat in its river valley as if it had done so for ever. There were no other fortresses like this one further west unless you travelled to the far end of Siluria and then crossed Oceanus to Hispania instead. Hidden deep in the interior of this landscape at the edge of the known world men were now lighting their oil lamps, preparing their food and gambling their pay on another throw of the dice. In these remote river valley forts, life would be little different tomorrow or the days or weeks thereafter.

A thud hit Attius' long oval shield as the blunt spear point bounced off.

'Good,' the instructor shouted, 'Now raise your spear and prepare to attack.' Attius did what he was told and the hasta fell harmlessly to the ground after bouncing off a defender's shield. 'Draw your sword and attack the straw Celt.' Again Attius steadied his mount and then launched his attack at speed. On a warmer day this would have been easy but with cold hands the sword slipped from his grasp falling to the floor. 'Pick it up later!' the instructor shouted: 'Next, form up to defend the baggage train from attack!' The small group rapidly assembled in good order pleasing their teacher. 'You have all shown an ability,' he said having them parade in a line before him. 'There is a little more drill for me to complete and then the time of your probation will be up. You will be sworn into your units and then sent out on your postings. That day will coincide with a display from an ala unit temporarily posted here to provide an example of mobility and spectacle not only to you but the legion as a whole. Nowhere in Britannia is it to be forgotten that peace has been hard won by the army. You will all witness the skills of your elders and learn from them. Also at their arrival you are to vacate your barracks and stables and then prepare a temporary camp outside the walls. These will be your defences so build them well as you have been shown. At their leaving you will dismantle the camp and be allowed to return. You have twenty days more practice so ask permission to go hunting whenever you can and avoid drinking at the bars. Stay close to the fort and do not stray far.' He then gave permission for them all to return to the stables as training for the day was over.

Attius gently pulled the iron helmet from his head. With cold hands he had struggled with untying the leather thong that kept the cheek pieces together across his face but the helmet came off carefully and was put to one side. Then bending forward he shook his back in waves of convulsions to force the chain mail armour to slip from his shoulders and into his waiting arms. It tugged at his hair and neck before surprising him with its weight. Wearing it had seemed easy. He stood up straight with his neck and head throbbing from tired muscles caused by the armour. Down his tunic ran the tell tale signs of grease and iron red stains from the wearing of it. He put his sword, now reclaimed, to one side along with the rest of his belongings, shield, spear and helmet and walked the short distance to complete the untacking of his horse, which had been silently and patiently standing still where Attius had left it tied up.

'Marcus Attius Octavianus?' a voice said.

Attius stopped his grooming and turned to face the inquisitor.

'Who are you? What do you want?' he said, muscles and thoughts already taught at receiving another unwelcome beating for a crime that he may or may not have committed.

A squat, tough legionary soldier faced him, totally unlike any of the thin legged horsemen that he normally mixed with. He was in his late thirties and, looking at his arm idly resting upon his sword pommel Attius could see that he was a veteran of many wars judging by the white scar tissue criss crossing his skin. In the sinews of that sword arm too he saw the strength that could punch a killing blow into any man's soft stomach.

'What are you doing here? They will not like it,' Attius said unsure of who 'they' were.

'If you are Attius, then I knew your father,' the stranger answered.

'Who was my father and what was his name?'

The soldier had a prominent nose and wore a short cropped beard. His eyes were blue and full of potential mischief. 'Your father's name is Julianus Falerius Silvanus. A good soldier,' he added to help win Attius over. 'How is he? I have heard that you are asking after me. So here I am.'

Although taller than the stranger before him Attius didn't want to square up to him and instead retreated to grooming his horse from a safe distance. From there the questioning continued.

'Listen to me. I am Gaius Macrius Sulla and a friend of your father's. I would like to be your friend too if you would let me!'

Attius hadn't been allowed to believe in friendships other than that with his slave Longinus. A new friend could trick you as fast as any enemy and just as deadly. 'My father is dead,' he said, hoping to kill their conversation.

At that revelation Macrius Sulla dropped his head and toyed with the bronze phallus pendant hanging from his belt. It was but a short while before he spoke again passing on his thoughts. 'May the spirits of the departed give him peace,' he offered, at which Attius struggled to prevent a tear from rolling across his face. Macrius moved a little closer and held the boy for a few moments until he felt that he was able to trust in him and then he stepped back a little.

'I've heard it said that you are having a difficult time. You have received regular beatings?' He asked. 'Is that true?'

'Nothing prepares you for this,' Attius replied, 'I'm learning.'

'And is your mother still alive?'

'As far as I know,' he replied thinking the question an odd one to ask. 'Why?'

Macrius Sulla was known to enjoy a drink and suggested that they meet later where they could talk in private about Falerius' death and other matters. He offered to pay for the entertainment and recognised that Attius hadn't done a lot of socialising since he had been enlisted. 'Meet me at the south gate later and if you like I will accompany you to find your slave,' he said and then left. Spirits raised by the unexpected visit of a potential ally, Attius cheerfully completed his final tasks for the day ensuring that his mount had hay and water for the night ahead. He watched as the beast slowly moved the hay about in his manger, selecting the best strands to eat. Attius was reminded of Roma and those days long gone when he and Longinus would ride across the soft hills pretending to guard the limits of the empire together. He looked forward to seeing him as it had been a while since he was forced to fend for himself and wished that his luck had been better. There was a little time for food and Attius took a bite at a hard loaf and some cheese before going to meet again with Macrius Sulla, his new friend.

Macrius was as good as his word and clapped his arm around Attius' shoulders before speaking the day's password to the guard; the arches passing high above their head as they made their way out towards the brief respite from military life. It felt warm and comfortable. A dimly lit street before them was short but full of tempting shadows, with meat already butchered hanging from the rafters ready for the night's pickings. People came and went from the alleys branching away from the main road, whilst others quietly went about decanting wine from larger storage vessels into smaller earthenware jugs to be put out on the broad shop counter. A gridiron placed above a peaceful charcoal fire bore the weight of three iron pots of stew that bubbled. Attius was keen to find Longinus before he could settle down for the evening and asked for his slave in all the open taverns. His investigations eventually bore fruit with the discovery of Longinus in the smoking kitchens of a friendly employer. The slave, he told Attius was a hard worker and loyal. The man had agreed to keep him on and although he wasn't his he would provide Longinus with food and shelter until Attius knew of his next posting and could take him along. To emphasise his authority over the shopkeeper Attius kept his recruit status to himself and gestured to Longinus to do likewise. He was in the cavalry and that was that. Macrius Sulla on the other hand was in the infantry and needed a drink suggesting a small room that he knew where the wine was good and women available for comfort's sake. It was here that Attius related the story of his father's death those short months ago.

He recalled how Cominius had filled his father with hope that the land may be valuable in time and how that wealth could be used to rise up the social order. Attius too, was to benefit in the future from his father's endeavours. He smiled at the thought of him showing the silver denarius to his mother with the promise of more to come. Attius lowered his voice to discreetly talk about the vast clay reserve and how it could be used to produce good woollen garments. There might be more there than the procurator would ever know about he managed to joke. He described the long term plans of his father's and how everything was to work out. That is before Gauis Helvius Bonus became involved. Macrius' ears were struggling with it all.

'Your father died over a ditch full of clay?' he said.

'Yes, no,' Attius stumbled to get out. 'It's not that simple. You see he was tricked. The beating I received for spreading rumours about the plague was meant to discover whether or not there had ever been any.'

'There's always sickness of some kind,' a bored Macrius replied.

'Well, they told me that Cominius, my father's friend here in Isca, had died of the plague and with that went his last ally. He was then tricked into having the land signed away.' Attius was struggling to get the apparent seriousness over to his supposed friend who at that moment was involved in ordering more drink.

'Do you know what Helvius needs, Attius? Do you? Riding a horse probably not! He needs some of this . . .' and Macrius simulated a well aimed blow into the soft stomach of his enemy with a sword. 'I'd do it myself,' he said.

'I've got other plans,' Attius said. 'I'm going to buy the land back.'

Macrius Sulla laughed louder than he had done for a long time and the others around them in the cramped drinking den lowered their voices to catch the reasoning for it. 'You're going to buy the land back? With what?' He questioned. 'Here we are waiting for a shipment of coin to arrive from Roma to pay us all and you want to save already? If the army aren't to steal it from you then the burial club dues will and what you don't drink and gamble away you expect to keep! You are free to ask for a posting to where you cannot spend anything but would the coinage ever reach you and therefore pay you for being there in the first place. This is the army Attius not a dinner table conversation. You have to fight for better silver and earn the right for it with promotion. Unfortunately there is no more fighting to be done. It is all over here. We are at peace. Look at Britannia on this coin. She is on guard with her shield and spear but against whom? The Emperor may leave you some in his will but don't expect it. After all he gave nothing away on becoming Emperor. We need a new one!' The last remark Macrius muttered quietly but was still audible enough for most to hear. A prostitute came close wanting to sooth the hurt on Attius' face but Macrius pushed her away. 'He'll want it for free,' he said.

Everything sounded all too familiar to the one struggling with the need to be there. Why all the training then and why all the soldiers? Attius felt crowded by the strong, brave, weak and cowardly all trying to drink that evening. The army united them all in a sense of purpose and life was as predictable as it could be, with its discipline and routine. Outside the military cloak people shivered in the unpredictability of what was to come and Macrius didn't care too much for them.

'Attius, we don't serve the people and we have no responsibility for them. We serve the Emperor, you too. It is his direction that we all follow and without any fighting he wishes that we build this province up stone by mason's cut stone. Those that aren't building are guarding those who are. You see all these men here? Well their wounds are from wielding the hammer and pick. Their muscles ache, Attius, as yours might and towards the end they are looking for due comfort in whichever way she arrives. Death will take you, Attius. Just don't ask too many questions of people and try to accept your lot. I'm sorry about your father but put the idea of land out of your head. There isn't any to be had.'

'But what of Longinus farming land for me whilst I serve?'

Macrius drank long and hard before finding the energy for another dinner table conversation. 'There are no guarantees Attius. I have already told you so and you cannot predict your first posting. As the army no longer takes from the natives then there will be no more to be had unless war returns. We might be too idle to fight then if we have to wait much longer. Your slave can fend for himself.'

The native beer soon lost its flavour and Attius couldn't drink enough of it to help blank out the present. Macrius instead saw him to his bunk and then, like the mysterious filthy god Charon, depositing the dead spirits on their predictable course through the Underworld, disappeared into the myriad of barrack blocks housing his own kind of soldier. He had gestured that he would be keeping an eye on the young man's progress but after his probation was up there was little else he could do. Attius would have to find a new friend or struggle.

CHAPTER X

GOLD

Into the blue skies of late April the Haruspex gleefully raised his warm bloody hands. On behalf of mankind it had been an excellent prophecy with the divining entrails laying there before him. Moving slowly he held them before his chest for all-conquering Jupiter to see from his lofty throne and, to a man, the entire garrison cheered wildly. Rome, backed by its armies, would safely continue in its quest to be master of the civilised world for another year at least.

'The men are in good spirits, Legate,' spoke the tribune in a good mood himself.

His superior nodded returning the compliment. 'They tend to believe in what they see and they believe that it is for real,' he said. 'Note that none of them are allowed to come too close for fear of contaminating this sacred place and its offerings. I discreetly selected them myself from a plate of three. Although not at war it does no harm to reassure the legion that mighty Jupiter is their protector and that Rome is invincible. She will still last twelve hundred years! This peace that we live under cannot last forever and we must remain prepared for war at the very least. There is an idleness about that can do us no good.' He had chosen his words carefully as the tribune had been sent to further his political career by serving in the armies across the empire and could return with his thoughts to the capitol itself. The Legate lowered his head towards the priest who retired gracefully a few steps backwards wiping the blood from his arms and allowing the commanding officer to step forward and address the troops himself. He raised his own arms into the sky for silence and spoke so that all could hear.

'Soldiers of Legio Secunda Augusta, you are in good heart and I share in your celebrations of the founding of Rome. We are far away here on the edge of our empire but mighty Jupiter still guards us across Oceanus, which has been calmed by Neptune's might for the noble roman cause. Nobody, least of all me, has forgotten you in your remote mountain outposts and, as I speak, other Legionary commanders are addressing their men in Eboracum and Deva. We share their fortunes both in war and in peace. Winter may have rested us but sadly I cannot call for you to sharpen your swords for another season in the field. War is over but the divine Hadrianus . . .'

There was the ripple of a roar throughout the massed ranks.

'The divine Hadrianus,' he continued, after allowing the warmth of affection to die down, 'wants us to build in stone and thus ensure that our empire will be ready to repel any foe that dares to challenge it. I doubt not your commitment to serve loyally and marvel at your skills. Your wall will stand as testament to our enduring mastery over these northern savages for many years to come. So may this day be victorious and victory to the army!' he shouted, before retreating to the rear of the dais and sitting high amongst his six legionary tribunes.

'What is the order of the day?' he asked the nearest.

'We will swear the new recruits in first. There will then be an artillery and legionary display followed at the end by an ala of Hispanics from Cicucium.'

'Excellent, then begin.'

'Marcus Attius Octavianus. Step forward.' He did as he was instructed. 'Now raise your right hand and follow in what I say to you.' Standing before Attius was the commanding officer of the legion's contingent of one hundred and twenty horsemen. Behind him stood the standard bearers on foot. All were resplendent in their mail and decorations. Attius in the excitement of it all couldn't recall everything that he had sworn on oath but briefly remembered to serve loyally and not to run away or abandon an officer. 'You are now accepted into the army Attius. Do you agree to obey?'

Attius wished that his father's spirit could abandon its lonely journey and join him that day. He raised his right arm again and was joined by the remaining troops. 'Idem in me!' they all shouted as one reaffirming their commitment to this army. His name would now officially be entered onto the army rolls and he would receive his pay. He retired backwards into the ranks allowing the next man to step forward and fortunately, as the army weren't conscripting masses of new troops, then the ceremonies would be kept short. 'Idem in me,' he reaffirmed at the right time. The next part of the day's activities could now begin.

The parade ground at Isca Silurum was certainly large enough to accommodate all there with a good view. Smaller ceremonies could be staged in the amphitheatre but larger shows arranged for the entire legion were best staged here. Not all cohorts were being called out to perform their drill and those chosen to do so went about it with efficiency, if a little slack following the idleness of winter. The Legate watched with interest as their colleagues rested upon spears propping up their shields. Water pitted iron helmets reflected Sol's brilliance and their red crests fluttered in a light breeze. Aeolus tugged at their shields and snaked amongst bare legs; white from the winter's sun. Hairs on their arms stood proud as they shivered slightly in the cool afternoon air, the smell of trodden grass and mud filling their nostrils.

The chosen men, having finished their drill, marched off to applause as the artillery wagons rumbled on pulled by labouring beasts. A driver rapidly urged his onwards and to go faster whilst their centurion barked for them to stop exactly where they were. Three men were to unload each machine from its cart, assemble it and then fire correctly at a straw target that had been erected some one hundred paces away by other unseen legionaries. There was a rush of activity as the men of the nearest crew laboured at their task and very shortly the machine was ready for its first shot. It creaked as the tension built up in the wooden frame reinforced with iron plates. Clunk, clunk the ratchet engaged and the senior legionary indicated with his bolt in hand whereabouts he wanted the machine's bowstring drawn back to. Adjacent to them another team had already loosened their bolt, which struck home with deadly force and accuracy. Its soldiers now stood back with grace to allow their colleagues to fire, whilst acutely aware of all the potential dangers at hand.

Attius watched in utter amazement having never seen the like before. The emperor could keep his fine buildings; who had built these? The Greeks, somebody sourly noted. Then Attius noticed something himself. The bow legged legionary looking along the sighting line of the weapon of war was none other than Macrius Sulla. He was sure of it. That deliberate stance of his was recognisable anywhere, not wasting effort in any way at all. In his hand he quietly held the thin leather firing cord and breathed confidently in. Attius willed the bolt to find its mark and thus leave his friend acclaimed as the best amongst them too.

The cord, once pulled, released the safety block allowing the bowstring grip to rise. The tension stored in the catapult's arms by having them pulled backwards via the ratchet would then be transferred into pulling the bolt forward at speed, before that energy in the bowstring was exhausted. Macrius pulled the cord and the arms flew forward with the bowstring and bolt. It landed harmlessly a few paces away point down in the soft earth. There was an enormous cry of laughter even from the dais that echoed across the flat river plain and around the surrounding hills beyond and back. A centurion rushed out and beat Macrius about his back. He tried to defend himself but backed away.

'Embarrass me and misfire again you fool and there'll be a flogging. Do you understand?' he said.

The centurion's brutality raised the suspicion of the Legate who got up out of his chair to get a closer look for he was as keen on the next shot as the soldier was. He shielded his eyes against the sun as Macrius again pointed to where he wanted the bow arms drawn back to only this time he chose to exceed the previous limit wishing the dart to fly faster and truer. He tapped at the frame with the next bolt in his hand as the two legionaries winding the ratchet backwards grimaced with fear. The whole machine appeared to creak more and they feared that the iron brackets holding it together would splinter along with the wood. They cowered as the machine reached its limit and were only too pleased to allow Macrius the pleasure of being solely alone with it when it fired. He stepped imperiously forward and raised the bolt to the sky before placing it tightly against the bowstring and then resumed the crouched position peering through the target finder. His Legate too leaned forward a little more whilst the Centurion picked his stick off the ground and held it tightly in both hands whilst fidgeting. Macrius Sulla then pulled the cord.

Attius remembered the silence that followed broken only by the cry of a soldier standing over his shattered weapon. For a second time the bolt had failed to release with the bowstring snapping under extreme tension. Attius remembered too seeing the Legate turn his back on events almost in acceptance that his Centurion was going to mete out ready justice in his way and without any need for authorisation from above. There then followed a rush and the vacuum of power quickly filled by the commander's bodyguard as the errant Macrius Sulla withdrew his gladius and charged like a madman the entire one hundred paces towards the straw man that had evaded his attempts at striking it with an artillery bolt. Pushing the target to the ground he firmly punched it in the stomach with his sword in much the same way as he had demonstrated in the tavern and having withdrawn it he then turned to face rapturous applause from all around, arms aloft.

'Is it over?' the Legate asked.

A horn sounded and the cavalry rode on at their signal just as Gaius Macrius Sulla was being unceremoniously dragged off. Their good mood prevailed too and having been sent to guard the mountain passes, they were now being deployed north to patrol the wild expanses of Caledonia. It was a new posting and this their chance to bid the west farewell with a fond cavalry display. In they cantered, in their turmae of thirty two men, all rocking to and fro in harmony from their saddles, spears held vertical to the sky in their right hands, shields in their left. Standard bearers and officers came at the head and wheeled round to take their salute from the Legate. Although a horseman himself he was keen to get back to the age old principles of an infantry army and set battles. Horses had their purpose but were unpredictable; a legion could stand its ground and fight. He politely acknowledged their presence however as he had done the army and retook his seat ready for the display to come. The horsemen turned and paired off; standard bearers were to stand their mounts quietly in one corner of the parade ground whilst the officers were to rejoin their men. At the signal given by a lituus, the cavalry horn, the first of the riders emerged from the massed ranks, their faces covered in silver masks. Attius had been told about this and edged a little closer for a better look forgetting to see where his friend had been dragged off to. A horseman flew close by and the feet of the spectators shuffled safely backwards. Another came close giving Attius the chance to see the rider's face mask more clearly and he could see that it was definitely that of a boy whereas others wore those depicting women. He sought an answer from amongst the more experienced there and was told that the display was to mimic the battles between the Greeks and the Amazons. Another rider passed by and discharged his spear with all the accuracy demanded by the crowd before wheeling around to rejoin his ranks. There were cheers as more and more came by in a similar fashion until the ground thundered under the soles of horses and the air shivered in a forest of yellow ostrich feather plumes. Silver pendants jangled from leather, freshly oiled to a deep bronze colour, hanging from the horses' sides, and iron mail rippled across its wearer's back. Finally it all stopped as quickly as it had begun and then silence. A Decurion rode forward coming to a stop before the dais. He spoke forcibly and with all the authority expected before placing his hand upon the sword pommel hanging at his right hand side beckoning the others to follow his lead. To a man they obeyed and in an instant withdrew their swords to the delight of Mars looking down from a cobalt sky. A salutation roared out:

'Salvete, salvete, salvete!'

Drawn swords were then returned to brightly dyed scabbards and the horsemen given their leave to return to barracks and rest. There would be feasting later that day as part of the celebrations and all could, if they so wished, attend to exchange insults and fight one another as they often did. Attius too would discover his own posting after the officers had reviewed their needs for replacements. He wished deeply for an ala destination but nothing would be decided until he was recalled back to the recruiting officer's room that afternoon. That gave him little time to worry for Gaius Macrius Sulla.

Attius closed the door without slamming it but wished that he had. Nobody amongst the recruits was going to be sent to an ala, but instead the legion had decided that its needs were best served by more horsemen for routine patrol work around Isca and escort duties to the gold mines out in the far west. They would all serve their time here in the barracks but Attius would be set to work ensuring the safe delivery of goods to the forts towards Luentinum. That would involve the regular contact with small garrisons at Cicucium and Alabum where supplies of food and weapons would be dropped off. It was uninspiring work but of a nature that wasn't regarded as dangerous and providing Attius didn't succumb to the harsh weather then life expectancy was good. The mounts weren't the best and neither was the pay but at least there might be the remote possibility of a visit home if peace continued. Ordinarily soldiers raised close weren't allowed to serve locally for fear of loyalties developing within the army and vicus. Attius ought to regard the posting as a good one and be thankful. Like all the others disappointed that day, he needed a drink and a fight if for no other reason than to prove his superiors wrong in their evaluation of his worth. A fight could elevate him in martial skills although any blow to his head could have been disastrous and he knew it. He headed for the taverns.

Various groups of soldiers were drinking quietly, their chatter of the day's artillery display and the expected punishment to come. There were no other horsemen there save for the odd legionary, who was happy for Attius to join him in the increasingly bitter taste of the local brewed beer. Yet one by one as his drinking friends deserted him for the richer pickings of a free meal following the feast, Attius, his money and spirits running low headed for his bed.

'What are you doing? This is my bunk. You horseshit are sleeping rough!' The soldier was one of a group in the room that Attius shared: A flagon of wine stood in the middle and around which four others were taking their drink. Their heads looked up at the unequal confrontation to come. It was five against one.

'So we are outside are we? I don't object to having to sleep without protection in the open skies,' Attius replied, 'but horseshit? What gives you the right?'

'Here . . .' And one of their number tossed a bronze sestersius towards him. 'Now clean my saddle and when you've finished you can clean my horse. After that take a message to your mother and tell her that I'll be riding to see her myself, messenger boy!'

'What do mean by messenger?'

'You asked for it . . .' and the Hispanic took a wild swing towards Attius' head where it connected throwing him to the ground. His vision blurred through the pain and drink had made getting to his feet difficult, but he recovered to deliver a telling blow of his own, before an oil lamp spilled of its contents caused the other assailants to stand back. The fight developed a little further and Attius felt the stabbing pains course throughout his body and in his mouth lay the taste of fresh blood. One good blow crushed his fingers as they connected with the hardness of his enemy's face, forcing him to squeal. A swelling began to rise from repeated attacks upon the weakest spot but Attius wouldn't give up. He rained blow after blow until forced away by the other four attackers join-ing forces, making a retreat inevitable. They rushed and pushed him towards the open doorway leading out into the narrow passageway between barracks, where Attius tripped and fell. Blow after blow from heavy cavalry boots landed upon his head until he began to lapse into unconsciousness. Fearing reprisals the four attackers left him there to hide inside their room wishing that he would regain enough strength to crawl off. A brief moment later and Attius was awake again. This was his chance to run but who was there for him? Getting carefully to his feet and using the doorframe for stability he looked down and noticed a bag lying there that he had tripped over in his haste to get out of the room. He couldn't make out its contents in the darkening gloom of evening but he snatched it up and began to run in any sickening confused way that he could towards his own camp.

'Who is it? Give the password.' The question came at the point of a spear.

'Marcus Attius Octavianus, recruit to the legionary cavalry. The password is "Aquila".'

'Enter Marcus Attius Octavianus.' and the spear dropped to the vertical. 'You know it's close to the last watch. I'd get to my tent if I were you. Now go!'

'Thank you.' Attius replied, bag in hand he squeezed through the small temporary gap that had opened in the thorn hedging barricade.

'I see that you have taken your food bag from the feast Attius. Is there enough there for two?'

Attius holding the bag up didn't panic. He had taken a beating for this, his prize and wasn't about to hand it over or suddenly get caught out but he knew what the guard had meant.

'I've been on duty most of this day Attius and everybody else has been arriving back in good time. Now, I've got hungry eyes that may or may not have seen you,' the guard said.

'Then I will buy you your meal. This one is unfit for the gods and therefore unfit for you too. Wouldn't you rather I bought you something better where you can choose?' Attius said. 'I'm so hungry that I cannot offend myself by eating old meat.'

'Forget the food, Attius. That will be a good coin in the morning then! Agreed?'

'Agreed.'

'Then get to your bed.'

Attius slipped into his tent and despite the various grunting and snoring noises of those around slept well for a man whose body ached more upon the hardest of ground. Through his blanket he shivered. Many older men would have walked away but for the young man lying there, it was his first victory. The stolen mask he could feel through the walls of the thin bag had been worth the risk and represented the booty of war. Soldiers stole and he was no different. Rolling it tight into his blanket Attius quietly waited for the morning call to sound and his orders for the day.

The dawn broke with the warmth that made everybody that more eager for their tasks. Yesterday's feast had been cleared away and the fortress returned to active duty. The task of the legionary cavalry was to take down their temporary small barricade, dismantle their camp and then report for appropriate duty. Attius quietly paid the night guard his coin and nothing more was said. A commotion had broken out in the barracks housing the Hispanics though. A valuable mask had been lost and there wasn't going to be time enough for a thorough search of the fort to find it, as the ala were due to reach their next camp that day. Their commander cursed the thief wildly, but it happened all the time. The night guards had been questioned about comings and goings but nobody had seen anything and therefore nothing could be proved. Among the horsemen it was a face mask, an item of great significance but not unusual. To any others it would stand out in its own right and be instantly recognisable; that made its recovery all the more likely, the tribune said. The ala missing a face mask therefore rode out of Isca through one gate, heading for their northern posting, whilst Attius on his lesser horse left the gate heading for the west and the tedium of convoy escort duties.

As the road bore them off towards the foothills he was drawn to a solitary figure picking away at the fort's massive walls. He strained his eyes to get a better view at what the figure was doing in broad daylight and was amazed at seeing Macrius Sulla. For his insolence the punishment had been to clear the drains and sewers of blockages and make sure that they were discharging correctly into the ditches. On a warm day as this it was unpleasant work and a cruel punishment for a worthy soldier. However there was nothing anybody could do and bribing somebody else to do the work instead was useless. Attius watched as the figure grew smaller and smaller its arms swaying from side to side as lumps of filth spurted out onto its legs and feet. There was a certain comedy to his punishment and the guards watching over him were keen that he suffered whilst they laughed.

After five miles or so the squeaking axle bearing from the cart was irritating the small escort especially those who were not asked to ride further out and cover the flanks for they were too far away to be bothered by it. The bright sun now rising into a clear sky beat down with warmth for the time of year and was making Attius thirsty. He requested a stop. The officer leading them wasn't keen and ordered the small procession of two carts and ten horsemen to continue until they were at least safe from potential ambush. Then they could rest and take a drink. He wanted to make the first fort by late afternoon, report their progress to the small garrison stationed there and deliver their cargo of iron, wheat and beer.

The roads were empty save for the occasional stragglers or beggars that the empire didn't care for. Too weak to be slaves and too poor to own anything of value they were allowed to beg their living from whomever passed them by. Attius' group spat at them before prodding them with their spear points. 'Who knows what diseases they carry,' the man alongside him said before lashing out with his boot at the beggars head. 'Get off the road and out of my way,' he growled. Throughout the day the pace slowed to a crawl and everybody felt the worse because of it. Although comfortable in themselves, the saddles had no way of allowing a rider to push his weight up and therefore out of the seat. At a slow pace the legs simply hung idly at the horse's side for mile after long mile. Their woollen tunics too, felt compressed by the weight of chain mail slapping at their stomachs with every step that the animal took and, where the flat shield hung across Attius' back he was sure that there would be a rub mark as there was on the saddle, where the two came into constant contact with the animal's every step, the bronze edging gradually cutting into the leather. To alleviate the boredom Attius began to count the stitches on the saddle and wondered at the maker's skill in producing such an item. Four horns, on a wooden frame for strength, covered in leather and padded by straw.

That game over and, unused to not returning to the fort for relaxation, Attius started to grow bored of the unchanging view. To start out it was an adventure but now everything had an air of familiarity about it. The road didn't select the most interesting path and instead chose the easiest gradient whether or not that appeared to be the shortest route. Another stretch led up a small valley to climb a ridge from where it descended to follow another valley before doing the same and so it went on. There were no villas and no towns here and little to speak of in the way of any occupation. The countryside around was wild and open with rough grasses, yet the small party stuck rigidly to the narrow road not wishing to leave its secure footing. Attius longed to be allowed to roam far and wide as he had done when growing up at home but now he had to cling to this gravelled surface in total obedience and not stray. On the horizon he spotted the remnants of an abandoned hill fort, long silent and still in the warmth of that spring day and wondered where the proud occupants had all now gone?

The fresh dewy air of the morning had dried out and the group needed to stop and take a drink with permission given to dismount. They chose to stop at a stream that ran with enough flow to ensure that the water would be clear and everybody without exception was glad to get off his mount and stretch. Nobody was to remove their armour though; helmets and chain mail were to be kept on. Shields could be removed to make bending easier for drinking. Horsemen were to take their fill first from the stream before allowing the draught animals down to crush the shallow banks with their weight and in doing so muddy the waters. Everybody was allowed a little time to rest here as the dangers were perceived as being few and, after all, the first of the forts was close at hand and a small contingent of foot soldiers may pass them by on their lonely patrol. The officer relaxed a little by picking at a piece of cheese from a bag whilst resting on the grass. Attius couldn't resist the temptation of having a look in his.

The leather rim of it was pierced and stitched over upon itself to accommodate a drawstring. The hide a beautiful golden tan which had seen many travels judging from its well worn appearance, although the mouth of the bag wasn't soft or saggy from over use in opening and closing. Attius pulled at this tightness and peered down inside. He could make out the mask from behind and was excited at how the metal smith had seemingly beaten a sheet of bronze about a face to form its shape and then silvered it for embellishment. He desperately wanted to remove it and push the cold metal against his own features for size. Would it fit and what would he see through the narrow eye slits of another's face? What was it like to breathe through the thin lips of the mouth unable to speak a word as its true owner had once done? He closed the bag tightly and put it back with his other possessions tying them onto the saddle.

With the call to remount some riders leapt back into their saddles although most too tired to do so chose to step onto a small hummock and fall into theirs instead. Positions were again taken up, with two men dispatched to riding wide of the road's boundaries on sentry duty. They would be the first to see an ambush at the edge but few expected it. However it was good practice and everybody, cheered by the small rest, began to talk as the carts rumbled their slow revolution towards Gobannium, where they arrived safely that afternoon greeted by an exchange of trumpet calls from the forts walls. The small force there were pleased to accept their supplies and, with no lack of space for either man or animal, the troops all slept well under the dark skies and Orion's watch. The province was at peace.

The following day continued in the same routine although they had further to travel to the next stop, Cicucium. After that it was another day to the gold mines at Luentinum, passing through Alabum, and then they would make the return journey. Again there were few stragglers on the road with the occasional cart slowly meeting them from the far horizon and then passing without discourse to disappear again in the opposite direction. Everything but the song of the wind spoke of silence. Attius, revelling in the openness of the place, enjoyed the stories of how the legions had marched in to create order from the wilderness, and how that order had left a barren empty land seemingly free of imperial interference. Their journey was as if it was just a dream, without purpose or substance, carried along the tiny roads of this province until their destination was to be revealed to them in a secret. That secret arrived two days hence in the form of the gold mines of Luentinum.

The mines were nothing like Attius or his friends had imagined. Falerius, secretly digging at his clay, had done so in such a way as to lull the suspicions of the local tax officer, who might want to assess its dubious value, but here, as in other places with imperial consent, there were to be no objections to the winning of precious metals. Vast resources of men, guarded over by a small contingent of soldiers, hacked away at the gold-bearing veins rippling across the hillside and, to provide the raw power required on this scale, water had been trapped miles away to be fed into huge chambers via aqueducts. From these the hydraulic power would be released through sluice gates to cascade down the hillsides, sweeping all vegetation out of the way and thus exposing the gold. In places the open mouths of caves that had already been sent to chase the metal stared out like death, the stale air from within lacking clean breath and from these, ragged souls emerged clutching their tools.

'Our camp is over there,' the officer said, pointing to the square turf and clay construction protected by a double ditch. 'Welcome to Luentinum,' he added, stopping short of describing its obvious lack of any amenities. 'We are to stay for one day only and then return to Isca. Apart from the gold there are several prisoners to return with.' The group relaxed before finally being given permission to remove their armour, after which they unsaddled their horses and turned them out to pasture in a small stone enclosed field close to the fort. Without exception all the beasts rolled in the fresh grass and ran about, before finally settling down to eat. Attius looked at the small guardian of the fort and wondered how something so unimposing could stand watch over something so precious. It didn't make sense. In discussing it briefly with one of the soldiers there, he was told that mining agents would eventually take over the operations under licence and that the military would move on elsewhere. There was no reason therefore to lavish the manpower and resources on building a larger more imposing fortress. Attius was seeing the empire at work. The empire that could choose to buy or seize land at will for its purpose of extracting every last monetary value from it, before seeking new riches elsewhere. The enemies of Rome may have died or run away but the insatiable appetite of its citizens for goods hadn't. He thought about his father's land and the procurator seizing it in the Emperor's name, and began to hate the swarms of workers crawling over this hillside. Why didn't they attempt to escape as the soldiers were so few and what was it that was keeping them here? Why were the goldsmiths working so obediently in their dingy workshops to produce pieces of such beauty? Attius grew confused at feeling this way for after all he was chasing the money himself.

The Centurion in charge appeared and showed them to their barracks, which were built of wood and not stone. He also showed them the ovens that they could use to prepare their evening meal and bake their loaves. However first the stores had to be unloaded and he would need a hand overseeing this as his men were busy with the mines. A small slave gang was organised and the task quickly completed; sacks of wheat and barley, small ingots of iron, amphora of beer and wine and olive oil all stashed away. The warehouse soon looked a lot healthier because of their journey and that would require repeating again and again along the same road at the same speed. If there was a harbour close by then that would save a lot of trouble but none was immediately available. Attius watched as the non-ambitious amongst the men rummaged through the sacks delighting in their delivery. Winter was always hard and they had come through it without having to pillage too much from the native tribes in order to feed themselves and every convoy was greeted with apparent joy. The small garden plot of the garrison was often the only available source of fresh food, although they had a granary in which dried stores were kept, luxuries were not out of the question but usually had to wait. The wheel marks that the carts made in the road would have no chance to fade away before the gold ran out, because Attius could predict having to come this way again and again, time after time.

That evening they all ate together. The slave camp was quiet and everybody settled around their food; the two senior officers of the camp and the cavalry discussing quietly what was new in Isca Silurum and beyond. There were no warm mosaic floors here, no fine dining rooms, but instead a simple hard existence coupled with the laxity of indiscipline. This could be a posting for life with year following year in endless cycles of boredom. There wasn't even an amphitheatre, no matter how small, to alleviate the painful existence of its guards. Attius wondered if, should a convoy fail to get through, would there be any news? The empire could be crumbling in the east and who would know or ever bother to send a rider to tell them? He tried to make light of the situation with the joke that on another day he would be returning with their silver and bronze pay chest only to be taking away the gold. He himself could grow rich on that trade! However the jocularity failed to find its mark as the ill educated had heard it all before and were resentful about receiving their money. Sometimes it turned up and sometimes it didn't. In order to defuse the situation the cavalry officer bade Attius to apologise and he would too. The youth was a new recruit and didn't know what he was saying, that's all. There could be no harm. With apologies accepted the men settled in for the night with gambling, drinking and a little womanising with those from the slave camp. There were pleasures to be had for little money and Attius wasn't going to say no to smelling the sweat of local women no matter how apparently disgusting. His problem was that money for him was running short and his next pay day was still months off.

The day for the return journey broke on a damp misty morning where shrouds of water bearing ghosts washed over the camp and all within it. For his ill thought out joking over their meal Attius was charged with organising the chain of prisoners that they were due to return with. He was curious as to why the mine could spare them and asked as to their fate.

'You are full of stupid questions!' a fat legged soldier answered. 'They are for the amphitheatre, animal bait. This has been their prison camp and now you are taking them for their sentence in the theatre at Isca. If you return and joke about my money again then I swear that you will be joining them in the next fight. Do you understand?' And with that he threw Attius the chain to which all had been attached with fetters around the neck and feet. The wretches from the underworld stood there shivering in the absence of work to keep them warm, and stared at the floor. Their fates couldn't have been any worse than enduring the harshness of digging in the airless mines and none spoke a word. Drops of water clung to them and their filthy attire and in Attius' cold hands momentarily hung their lives. From the depths of evil Tartarus they were to receive their punishment from him and others like him.

'Get up,' he said 'Into the wagon,' pulling them to initiate their total obedience through pain. They did as he had gestured and one by one slowly clambered aboard the cart, its back open to allow them in. He looked at them and castigated any trying to proclaim his innocence. 'It's too late,' he said with the authority invested in him remembering how Longinus would select the fattest ewe for market without compassion. There was always a time to die and this was going to be theirs.

'Attius?' There was a weak whisper from the next man boarding. 'Are you Marcus Attius Octavianus, son of Julianus Falerius Silvanus? You look familiar.'

'Why do you ask?' Attius replied, almost ready to repel the stranger with some form of violence at hand.

'I am Julius Cominius Civilis, friend to your father. The land Attius, remember the land. You were young then but I helped your father buy his farm. Now you have to help me. I am going to be killed.' His voice, barely breaking through cracked lips, was unfortunately audible to most of the others. 'Tell them that I wasn't trying to cheat the Procurator and that I will pay them back. Tell them Attius!'

'How can I help you? This is nothing to do with me. My father is dead.'

The other prisoners on the wagon soon began to realise that in hushed conversation Attius could be their saviour too, the weak link, and raised their voices. 'You've agreed to help him now help us too,' they pleaded their cries bringing unwanted attention.

'Attius! What are you doing? Why are you talking to the prisoner?' the Centurion asked.

'This man is mistaken. He thinks that he may know me,' Attius replied pointing in the direction of the condemned man.

'I hope not, Attius. That man is Julius Cominius Civilis and he has been found guilty of stealing from the Emperor in using his rank in the army. We've confiscated the monies we could find and seized any land that he had bought that we can trace. He and his family have been disgraced, he has been written from the army records and this is his final journey after he tried to escape. Now don't stand too close to him and get them on board. Hurry up!'

A dull cry called for the Centurion to look around and see a man on the floor with the chain taut and the others attached to it struggling to remain on their feet.

'Attius!' he cried.

'Sorry. I am trying to be a soldier,' he weakly said and with that he helped Cominius into the wagon and towards his fate.

The party mounted and set off for Isca shortly after dawn. Their horses, groomed by slaves, were already saddled for them and the axle bearings greased so as to run silently. Ahead lay the cloud laden mountains that the road was making for and Attius, the cold damp wind blowing about his neck, was suffering a headache with the tightening of his shoulders. He drew the cloak about himself, cursing his mount as it jogged on at the slightest release of pressure on its reins. He shouted 'Stand still!!' knowing that the animal had enjoyed its rest more than he had and it obstinately obeyed. There was the boredom of many miles of straight road to come that Attius hoped would temper its spirit. His hands too were cold but these he successfully managed to tuck into the folds of the thick wool before the animal realised that control over its mouth had been momentarily given up and then regained. Permission had been refused for Attius to ride further out on scouting duties; it was a responsible job requiring experienced eyes and he would be needed closer to the wagons for the attack that all knew was never going to come. The scouting would have meant bodily movement and therefore warmth, as well as the added interest of riding over different terrain compared to a road surface of whatever material happened to be locally available. Attius could only think about what he was doing there when at home Gaius Helvius Bonus was enjoying the profits of his father's work. What too of the surprise of finding Julius Cominius Civilis his prisoner? It couldn't be any stranger, although Attius had noticed Cominius' army name tag was missing from around his neck, possibly ripped from him by his superiors or simply thrown away at his escape as a disguise. No matter, as an educated man wasn't going to be able to hide amongst the illiterate tribesmen for long he was soon offered up by them through fear of reprisal.

Through the bars of his prison cage the ex-engineer continued to protest his innocence and bemoaned his treatment.

'Talk to him,' he shouted in obvious discomfort at getting the words out of a sore throat and pointing at Attius with thin arms. 'He knows more than he's saying and I knew his father. Why don't you ask him? It isn't only me involved in this!'

The officer there obliged out of curiosity and rode alongside Attius.

'He says that he knows you.'

'He knew my father and therefore of his family. He doesn't know me.'

'Did your father deal with this man Attius?'

'I don't know. My father is dead and I have never seen him on our land before.'

'Was it your land, Attius? Didn't you inherit when your father died and why did you arrive with such a glowing recommendation?'

To avoid unnecessary complications the pair separated away from the cart and Attius began to explain how his father was finding it hard to sell his wool in the markets around at the time of his death. Therefore he had sold the farm to a local wealthy businessman to avoid further ruin. There was no land left for Attius to return to and no home. He wouldn't elaborate on his mother's whereabouts; suffice to say, that with the gods' protection he was sure that she was still alive. Not entirely convinced by the story the officer nevertheless was sorry to have heard of Falerius' death. 'You have to join up early to get anything from this life and even then death can devour you at any moment,' he said and rode on, leaving Attius alone with his old thoughts. In the cart lay an able bodied soldier who in war would have been demoted but forced to fight for the very existence of this province. In peace however he was seen as a criminal and counted for nothing. Every day Attius grew a little more resentful at his lot and that of the others in his company, wishing he were home.

'Attius, listen to me.' The pleas resumed from the cage. 'If I'm to die then let it be with the sun upon my face and the breeze drifting through the branches of the forest. Let another find me cold with death and commit my body to the earth by placing soil upon my empty eyes. I don't want to die in fear, Attius, by watching it arrive. Can't you understand? Help me escape! I'm no soldier and I have nothing to give you. What pleasure is there seeing a broken man fighting for his life? What can my death mean to you? What can it mean?'

Attius had heard enough and kicking his horse hard in the right of its rib cage caused it to veer violently to the left and towards the wagon. With his shield boss clutched tightly in his hand he slammed it hard into the soft fingers poking out to grasp at the free air outside its confinement causing the man to squeal and return to his place.

'Speed up!' Attius ordered the wagon driver. 'May your wheels drown him out so that none can hear his crying. Onwards: to Isca!'

Nobody was to request stopping over the next few days for anything other than the necessary relief of bodily functions, and the weather, which had been normal helped force them on. Hills which had been hills on the way out suddenly took on growth in the low clouds shielding them squeezing the road in its valley confines to little more than a path. Eventually the small cargo of rich golden yellow mineral wealth and rotting human flesh dropped down and towards the easier gradient to Isca where the fort and its amphitheatre of death lay in wait.

Signals were exchanged and with the guard satisfied that they were who they said they were allowed them to enter. Wearily, helpers were instructed to unload the carts outside the fort's strong room, where the gold and human cargo would be hidden away from human eyes. Attius would be allowed to rest for a couple of days prior to having to return for more gold and so it would go on. He had realised that this was going to be his lot. Macrius Sulla inevitably sought him out though, and over a drink, the two men joked at having somebody poke the turds from the arses of fools as they sat on the latrine. However with more drink flowing Macrius became increasingly bitter.

'Those bastards!' he said. 'They will pay a price for that punishment. I may joke but shit stinks and there are better punishments than that for a man with my record.'

'Better than death itself?' replied Attius, who then went on to tell him about Cominius and his dealing with Falerius, although sparing a few details in case his friend's drinking anger caused him to repeat something that he may regret later.

Below the floor of the one room sacred to all soldiers, the room where the standards were kept and where the gods of war and fortune lived, fifteen bodies lay twitching in their darkened cell. Next to them in another ante room was the gold, securely locked away in its chests that they had helped win from the wild land. That precious metal, the reward for all conquests, would soon be released to shine in the brightest light of many days; at the same time those fifteen bodies would lay twitching in the sun, their rich red blood staining the sand of the arena for entertainment under flowing banners of purple.

CHAPTER XI

THE DECISION TO RUN

With the orchestra playing on, a weak Cominius died a braver death than even he could have imagined, sent to the crowded banks of the Styx by a cheering mass. There he would idle before Charon chose him to cross. Pluto wouldn't claim him for he was marked as unrighteous and there were braver, better men to go in his place: men that their ancestors could be proud of.

Under the warm October sunshine the first wolf emerged into that small intimate arena. It could not find sanctuary from its tormentors and slunk close to the circular wall for safety. It was confused, hungry and appeared to lack the strength within it to kill anything but a creature smaller than itself. How was it going to kill Cominius? Man upon man in the rows bayed for him to attack first and the two eyed each other with caution. Cominius, taking his chance, threw his spear and in claiming to not be a soldier was found to be a liar, the spear hitting its mark and downing the creature. He moved closer to the wounded animal, oblivious to the shouting and horn blowing about him and looked the wolf in its eyes. He had never been this close to a wild animal before and would have taken pity upon its plight at any other time. The blue eyes of the creature stared back as it dragged its hind legs behind it in an attempt to escape further punishment, the spear firmly lodged in its side. From its damp sand matted coat, red blood seeped out and it whimpered loudly enough for Cominius to hear above the noise.

'Kill it!' somebody shouted and Cominius looked up into the clear sky before momentarily raising his shield above its head and then smashing it down with all his strength into the unprotected face of the wolf. A soft crunch broke its skull and left it to die.

Everything spun around and although barely armoured Cominius was finding the sand arena difficult to tread. He fought hard for his breath aware that through one door another three wolves were being sent against him. Quickly snatching his spear from the dead animal's side he regained his posture of fear. How many did he have to kill before being pardoned? How was he going to escape from this? The three new adversaries were braver than the last, hunting as a pack, and slouched seemingly as disinterested in their prey as they were in the crowded banks around. Cominius moved his body with them. If they turned so did he and he refused to allow them to get behind him. Trying to watch all three at once became tiring and having thrown his spear and missed, he drew his sword and waited for their first attack. It wasn't long in coming and the sword successfully sunk into the throat of the first, spraying flecks of blood into Cominius' warm face as the beast's teeth passed by. He instinctively wiped at it whilst the second animal tried to pull him down by tugging at his leg. He swiped at the biting animal and missed at which the third leapt at him grabbing him by the neck and severing his artery. There was no time to cry to the gods for their hearing and, after a short convulsion, Cominius' spirit departed its empty body. Attendants sent in with flaming torches drove the animals back from their kill. Rome had had her justice.

Cominius' body was claimed by nobody and along with the other carcasses of the dead was thrown into a pit. Without pain or pleasure, Attius had watched it all, choosing to leave before another of the fifteen were sent in. Outside the eroticism of death was touted for by prostitutes wanting to console those witnessing the fickle fate of life. They clung to the entrances and waited for their moment, Attius passing them by on his way to find somewhere quieter. He despised human contact and looking at the small fields surrounding the fort made for the grazing animals of the cavalry, heads down in contentment or sleeping in the warmth provided by Sol. A cheer rose from behind him announcing another death and a cloud momentarily filled the sky.

The horse grazed at will as he approached hand outstretched for it to sniff. It had kind eyes and didn't appear too disturbed at not being given any food and returned to lowering its neck and chewing at the grass before it. Attius looked at it carefully. The legs were straight and strong but the back weak with length. The neck was thick but the chest too small. It was good natured and responded kindly to having its neck rubbed and coat stroked. Attius patted it and estimated it to be about six or seven years old and not one that he had been given to ride.

'A true horseman, Attius. You neglect human company?'

The voice by his side came from one of the legionary tribunes, a man finely regaled in a clean tunic and robe bearing the purple stripe of his rank. His stout leather boots had made no sound on their approach as had neither of his bodyguard's armour, hands on the pommels of their swords as they shielded him from potential harm.

'I take it that you witnessed the brave death of our friend Cominius?'

'Yes, Tribune, I did'

'And there is no other sport there today to tempt you into staying, Attius? After all, in this peace that we are living under it is important to see a man push a sword into another's flesh and glory at how he dies. You smell the blood of your enemy and Cominius was such an enemy. Do you not agree?'

There was no reply to give.

The tribune continued. 'Before allowing him this moment of personal glory in front of the fates, he spoke, of you. We will have to investigate what he told us, along with what your commanding officer himself has reported. If it is true then we will have to look at taking it to the Governor or Procurator to investigate. Theft is frowned on and your family and land is in peril. Are you sure that you have told us the truth.'

'Tribune,' Attius said, 'I have told you everything. My reference was excellent and I look forward to a long and successful career here in the service of Rome and her armies. I am enjoying my new life and if there is any wrongdoing then it is not of my making. I have no lands or family to return to, my father is dead and my mother I do not know of.'

'Your reference from Gaius Helvius Bonus? Is he still alive and where is he a magistrate? I will need to talk to him. You see Attius, however good a soldier you may profess to be we can pick the best at the moment and do not need to rely upon drafts to fill the ranks. If you are guilty of wrongdoing then you will be punished and dismissed from the army. Cominius, to his fault was already serving and therefore died a soldier's death. I want you to stay close to the fort for now and not to ride out with the gold escort. Do you understand?'

'Yes. I understand.'

With a nod the Tribune turned about and headed back towards the games and their killing. It was still early in the day and there were better fights to come. Attius watched him swagger off and had to take heed of what he said. He was a suspect for having done what? Nobody was dead except his father. From the gates in the low walls of the amphitheatre Attius watched as a few people began to drift away, mostly those who lacked the twin courage of withstanding the stench of human entrails laid bare and thick incense to disguise them. One such person making his exit was Longinus, not out of any displeasure but out of the need to return to his work. The day's spectacle had been free and many slaves keen to provide an audience to witness Roman killing Roman. The day was about to return to its monotonous self until across the grass ran Attius towards him.

'Longinus, stop!' He shouted. The slave did as he was told and in a breathless rush of excitement that caused him to pause before the next sentence, Attius added 'I have some work for you.'

'Master Attius. It's been a while since you had need of me. Where have you been? Have you seen the games?'

'Yes. Now I need you to do something for me.' There was urgency in the young man's voice that concerned the slave, for it could lead to his possible harm and Longinus shunned danger.

'What is it you wish me to do?' he said.

Attius looked about him. He didn't want to be overheard.

'I want you to leave your job quietly,' he said. 'Make up a story and say that you have work elsewhere. Find yourself a horse and return to see my mother any way that you can. Be quiet in your travels and stay out of sight especially around Durocornovium. Do you understand? You are to see her alone and say "Fortuna grants her the wish". There may be others,' and with that he thrust a pouch of money into his hand. 'Spend little,' he added, 'as I have no more pay to come this year. I will expect you back before the snows of winter arrive and remember, you must not be seen by Helvius, Cornix or Tancorix. Now go!'

Longinus, although excited by the task given him and the chance to see Julia again, was less than happy at having to travel at that time of year. It was going to be cold and difficult and for him; he wasn't as young as he used to be. Nevertheless there was a trust placed in him although he was unsure at Attius having the authority to speak for the god or goddess Fortuna. It was his master that needed protection he felt. Slipping away into the throng heading for the alternate entertainment of the vicus, Longinus left Attius with people passing him by busy with talk of the morning's work and declaring their intention of returning later to witness the real killings of the day and proper gladiators.

Attius too needed to speak to Macrius Sulla and would have been dismayed to have found him there in the front row of the theatre so close as to get a good view of the last death pangs of the condemned. Yet having seen combat himself, Macrius had a need to relive the closeness of death and glory in, that no matter how violent it was, he couldn't be harmed. All the old memories came rushing back and the ghosts of the dead appeared to dance on the arena floor where they died a quieter death before fading away. Attius had no intention of joining them: no man was ever going to condemn him to the same fate, yet out of servitude he returned to his seat and watched on impassively.

Six weeks of increasingly colder weather meant that fewer escorts were being sent to the mines. Looking for the precious metal in such conditions was difficult enough in the darkening days without the added expense of providing more light for the miners to work by. They were moved elsewhere to undertake other tasks requiring obedience and servitude. The games had depleted the numbers of those condemned and nobody was going to risk their life unnecessarily in order to add to the role call for the next spectacle. The roads too were slowly being closed down and traffic was scarce in its comings and goings, so much so that the entire garrison was seemingly hemmed in by the weather, prisoners of the cold behind their stark walls.

Longinus hadn't returned and neither had the inevitable agents sent out to talk to Gaius Helvius Bonus. Attius grew worried and impatient at the lack of information. There was a legion at full strength bored at its confinement and how he longed for mutiny so that he could escape his ordeal and return home. It wasn't to be and soon Saturn brought his festivities to the time of year where everyone would have to parade before the standards safely locked away and renew their loyalty to them and to the Emperor Hadrianus. They all longed for news of a campaign season but the rumours told otherwise. There had been fighting in Judea but it hadn't required reinforcement to help. The situation was under control and the province of Britannia remained at peace and stagnation. It was as the emperor wished and everybody obeyed. Attius obeyed too, following routine until the day the Centurion sought him out.

'Attius I am going to kill Valerius. Will you help? After all you have little to lose yourself.'

'Keep your voice down, Macrius, you fool,' Attius replied, crouching low to the bread oven for warmth. He pulled his cloak over his head and moved closer to the heat. 'Why are you going to kill him?'

'He's greedy and I've had enough of the punishments that he is giving out. I'm a proud man, as your father would have known, and have fought hard for this legion but I'm not going to be somebody's slave forever. He is hated by everybody and I'm going to finish it, if not for them.'

Attius groaned at the sense of it all. 'Why not take him in a dark street with your dagger?' he asked.

'For fear that everyone will be blamed if nobody came forward to admit the killing and that punishment would fall on them all. The best time is coming up at the oath taking where in the confusion it will be hard to point the finger at anyone. That will be my chance and I could escape.'

'Macrius, why don't you simply run away and risk being tried as a deserter if caught?' Attius asked.

'No. I am a soldier and I will face a soldier's death if caught.'

Without Longinus, without news of his mother and with the prospect of being found culpable along with Cominius, what did Attius have to lose? He poked at a flat loaf of bread, scooping the others out before they went cold in the air. 'I have to take these inside. I'm on oven duty but help yourself to a piece, then you can tell me more,' he said. A cloaked and secretive Macrius waited for his friend to return from the row of barrack blocks directly behind the rampart. Without doubt there were many plotting to escape that winter from their military servitude. For others, the routine and harsh discipline suited, serving its purpose.

Attius returned, the white snow balling up under the hobnailed soles of his boots. Crouching low he put more wood in the oven and poked at the embers causing a spark to all too briefly float into life before spinning and then disappearing into the dark throat of the chimney.

'Vesta keeps up warm,' he said trying to avoid any talk of killing but broke down in curiosity. 'Exactly how are you going to take Valerius?' He was unsure of his part in the plot.

'By arrow and from a distance,' Macrius replied.

'Then I cannot join you. The idea is ridiculous as you cannot fire a catapult without it breaking.'

'Friend', said Macrius Sulla, 'the arrow will be true. I've had practice with the auxiliaries whilst on patrol with them and have brought down game with ease. I know that I can do it. I also have a bow hidden away,' and he smiled.

Attius was still concerned as to why his help would be needed to which Macrius answered 'You've nothing here. No promotions, no favours and no friends. You're sent out on escort duties whilst others stay here and grow idle at your expense. So join with me and escape. By firing an arrow they won't know from where it came and will panic. I need you to man a boat for me in which there will be time to escape to Sabrina Fluvius and then across to Durotrigia where we will find shelter with my family at Lindinis. From there you are free. The garrison here will be looking for a tribesman or ambush and will relish the prospect of raiding the local villages in searching for retribution. Think Attius, there is nothing new in us taking a Roman's life.' It sounded all too easy.

'The garrison here will soon find us and what about the fleet patrolling the crossing?'

Macrius didn't answer but with the stopping of the snow the heavens briefly parted to allow the gods a view upon man's activities. Who was it that listened that night to their hushed conversation?

Saturnalia came and went in its rituals with the old Saturn dying and the new Saturn being reborn into the world and, with their reaffirmation of those loyalties to both emperor and standards completed, a legion that was now at peace busied itself for a visit from Publius Mummius Sisenna, the governor of Britannia. Although early in the year for comfortable travel, Sisenna was keen to report back to Rome upon the many building projects started in the province following Hadrianus' visit many years before. Coming to Venta had been of particular interest to Sisenna as the town had developed unusually in comparison to the others he had seen in the province. It lay east of the major fortress of Isca Silurum and was seemingly unconnected to it, as if the whole crowded vicus normally found outside a fortress had picked itself up and moved to virgin ground elsewhere and started its own development. Upon this part of Britannia the snows were quietly settling deep in peace.

Although without ditches and despite an incomplete internal road system, Sisenna and his advisors had decided that the risk of attack was small and therefore would keep his visit to the Forum quiet. He would meet the local tribal leaders and address any problems in the nature of his office, and then inspect the building works for himself without the usual baggage train of his bodyguard following on. To accompany him there was only going to be a handpicked selection of centurions amongst whom was Valerius. These men were to stand at a watchful but respectful distance as the governor and his scribes noted down what had been achieved and what was left to be achieved. In the event of danger they would close in and protect Sisenna with their own lives whilst riders would summon help from the nearby fortress. It was to be a relaxing visit and one free of excessive troop concentrations, men who may have outnumbered the very inhabitants choosing to set up home there already. If the town was to grow then the army had to be part of its past and not its future, save of course for any monies that off duty soldiers spent there, or the use of military masons and engineers to supervise the local workforce in their constructions. War was not a word to be uttered here for after the long and bitter years of fighting, the hillforts of Siluria had been emptied of their occupants and new opportunities opened for them to live peacefully in the emerging towns. Sisenna knew that, drawn to these centres of administration they could be watched over, counted and taxed. Hopefully they would continue to arrive as natives but eventually settle as Romans.

It wasn't the time of year for an ambush; without foliage for cover and with tracks being easily followed in the snow. Macrius Sulla had made a military mistake as he lay in a small hollow, his hands shivering with the cold and wrapped tightly in his cloak.

'What can you see?' Attius asked.

Macrius, one knee on the cold hard ground, peered over the rise before him. Below, the road passed by and although not oblivious to its surroundings, kept a well ordered distance from the wooded banks beyond. 'The road's empty,' he replied. 'It looks as if the main group are still in the town. There's a standard there and I can see a small horse guard moving around. How much more is there for him to see? If they remain any longer they will end up staying the whole night and there is nothing there!'

'And you are sure that Valerius was sent with them?' Attius continued.

'Yes, I checked the day's rota before I could manage to escape.'

'Good.'

Next to Attius lay Longinus looking even colder than the others. He was now very weak and had returned to Isca barely two days since after delivering Attius' coded message to his mother. He had seen Julia himself but had not reported any news of imperial agents on the farm. The journey for him had taken its toll and he appeared close to death, not having had sufficient money for either food or sleep over the weeks he had been away. His horse too had been struck with foot rot lameness as excessive rains had made the road verges impassable and everyone travelling was using the harder road surface. On many occasions he had to dismount and then lead the animal by his side, which ate into the days he had been away. Attius had asked a lot of his slave yet Macrius proved understanding in his acceptance of why he had to come along on this most foolish of missions.

To counter the look of distain upon his friend's face the soldier explained again that there was no going back and that if they were unexpectedly separated then to make for Lindinis and his family there.

'Macrius, quick!' Attius said having taken another look at the town. 'I think they will be forming up soon to leave. The horn has sounded. If Valerius is in the vanguard then you will not have to risk hitting any others.'

Macrius crawled to the point of risking himself being seen and calculated how long it would take for the group to come within range. Two hundred paces he estimated. Attius thought more like one hundred if he was to get a good shot off. There would only be the one chance in this. 'Try to aim for the front where his shield cannot save him and remember he won't be expecting it,' he whispered.

'Get your slave and tell him to start running. We'll catch him up.'

Attius, pulling Longinus to his feet thrust a bag into his arms containing his father's sword and the stolen cavalry face mask. Pushing him forcibly into the woods behind he let 'Don't come back' suffice.

One thousand paces away, the small detachment of soldiers had already started out from Venta along the road towards Isca. At their head solemnly marched Valerius, tasked with leading the group home following their visit. His shield correctly hung from his left arm whilst his right hand rested on his sword pommel. Following him came the governor's small guard, which had spilled off the road looking for potential targets. Nobody expected anything. Attius nervously thumbed a coin between his fingers portraying the head of the emperor. It wasn't him they were about to potentially attack but Publius Mummius Sisenna, his governor.

'Macrius, let's stop this. There is time and it's full of danger. We have an opportunity of returning to the fort before we are missed.'

'No. My time is now. Run with your slave if you want!'

The party was now barely fifty paces from them and making good speed in the snow. Considering the lateness of the afternoon and the light, their guard appeared to be down as a stranger leapt from the banks bow in hand. Pushing his cloak off his shoulders he fired before they raised their shields in a protective cordon about the governor. An arrow whistled amongst them and embedded itself in a man's guts. He clutched at it before slumping to the ground. As the party formed its protective shield a trumpet blared out into the cold afternoon sky, followed by two horsemen rapidly making for the direction of Isca. Another arrow fell amongst them. Two other horsemen chased Macrius Sulla into the woods, their spears falling short of bringing him down. Fearful of more archers they kept their distance marking the spot for others to follow in numbers and strength.

Attius panicked. In a few brief moments of madness there had been three of them sharing the danger. Now there was only him. Other soldiers realising that the immediate attack was over began to nervously spread from the road towards where he lay. He could be found cowering there and no amount of explanations would ever save his life. Turning he ran too and didn't stop. On the ground behind him a coin lay cold from its human contact, the bearded face of Hadrianus looking in the direction to which the assassins were headed.

It didn't take him long to catch Longinus. Knowing that within the space of the remaining hours of the day a huge search would be out looking for them, as they struggled for their miserable lives, planning to make for the coast and obtain the short sea crossing to Durotrigia. However in the darkness it was becoming harder to negotiate their way and, in need of shelter from the bitter night, came across a disused stone hut. Attius withdrew his sword and went in first. There had been evidence of iron working although the iron was missing. Instead stacked in one corner was a small supply of black rock that had been used in other fires. In the gloom he managed to get a fire started pleading with Vesta to provide warmth for them both. 'I shall repay you,' Attius vowed and after making the hut a little more comfortable saw to his friend Longinus. The slave was barely conscious and was obviously going to find it hard going on any further. Even if they survived this night there were going to be many more of similar peril. Attius wrapped him tighter within his cloak gently moving him towards the flickering life of the flame. The black rock burnt with a peculiar smell and hoping not to be betrayed by it, he went outside to see if its odour carried in the wind. Fortune was with them for there was little evidence of them being there and no glow came from within the small building. He remained on guard, eventually returning inside as the first of the morning light broke and hoped that the chance for sleep would have raised his slave's spirits for the day to come. Longinus still lay where he had been left, having not turned in his sleep. Attius coughed at the smell still coming from the dying fire, his eyes streaming.

'Wake up,' he said prodding Longinus in the foot. 'We have to go. How did you manage to sleep with this smell? Come on. We have to get going.' He prodded him a second time yet the body on the floor couldn't move. He was apparently still fast asleep.

The loyal family slave had died there, his face pale in the morning light, his eyes closed in sleep for their final time. Attius shook him violently. 'No!' he cried, 'Not now! Wake up, wake up!' but there was no reply. Although his spirit was close by, Longinus too had gone.

Attius, full of fear with the dead so close, snatched the bag up and ran. Everything was now a foe – the countryside, its people, its gods and more importantly the great river that was barring his escape home. What was he going to do without Macrius and now without Longinus. In what direction was he heading? He didn't know. With these decisions he wanted to sleep soundly in a warm bed and then wake refreshed ready to make the right one, yet sleep was going to be a long time in the coming. His mind tired from its labours had to fight on and his body aching from its toil would find little rest either.

Having run south for what seemed a long time Attius began to sense the closeness of water and hear it upon the wind in its rhythms. He cautiously looked out from the woods and up and down the river bank searching for signs of life, military life especially. There was none, but out on the water a ship moved silently in its passage upstream. Not wanting to be seen he withdrew into the cover and waited for it to go. There was little time to waste looking for a crossing as with every hour the garrison of Isca could be out looking for him, so he came out of hiding and moved upstream until someone sitting by a fire caused him to stop. There a fisherman ate his breakfast with his boat idling in the tidal water. Attius quietly opened his bag and again withdrew the blade that had been his father's and with the fisherman's back turned, he took his chance and broke cover, brandishing the sword.

'You! I need your boat,' he threatened.

The fisherman taken by surprise turned to see Attius standing there.

'Come warm yourself,' he said. 'It's cold out here. Are you on the run from the military? You wouldn't be the first. Come . . .' and he beckoned Attius towards the clear flames of a crisp fire. Attius warily approached sword in hand, and accepted a piece of cooked fish.

'You're scared,' the man continued. 'Have you any plans? Where are you heading?'

In trying to speak too fast Attius blurted out that he wanted to be taken across the river to the other bank.

'Not until the river has filled and then settled a bit. It's too dangerous otherwise. It's going to be an hour's time.'

'Now!' Attius shouted stepping forward and waving the sword at the fisherman. 'Now!'

The fisherman could see the anxiety in him. 'Kill me, then,' he said. 'There are no others to take you across and it's a long walk to cross further upstream. You can wait with me or you can walk.' Up to now it was the longest hour of the young man's life. An hour when Macrius Sulla could successfully emerge from the woods onto the shoreline and in unbelievable detail, reveal how he managed to escape the pursuing army. In the hour Attius could reflect on his being there. How had it come to this? Little by little every wave grew in size, striking the eroded bank where the two men sat, barely a word between them, and time passed slowly.

'That's it we can go,' the fisherman said, having had his eyes on the water for what had seemed a lifetime. 'Put your sword away and give me some help.'

Attius, keeping the weapon in view, climbed in after him and watched as the sailor skilfully turned the boat around into the wind. With the sail raised he allowed it to glide into the deeper water. No alarms sounded from the shore line and no figures ran out, but in a winter's sky the sail flapped and the boat gently rose and fell in its passage towards the distant snow capped hills of Durotrigia.

CHAPTER XII

THE SEARCH FOR ATTIUS

With the cold came the loss in weight. Attius had let the fisherman keep his life in return for what he could show him to eat on the shoreline and it was with this scavenger's dinner that he kept himself alive. Out on the grey sea, boats came and went but none had discharged Macrius upon the same beach that Attius had found himself upon. In losing count of the number of days that he had decided to wait it was going to be hunger that eventually drove him inland and not merely disloyalty to his errant friend. His head too had now cleared of its sickness brought by the waves and with returning strength he stood up, looked out over the vacant space and wished Macrius luck. Into the wind he muttered 'I have nothing, I can offer nothing.'

Perhaps the army had quickly caught him and Macrius had kept his mouth shut. Men ran away all the time and the fisherman knew it too. Attius may have regarded himself as free in being a deserter but although his height could give him away, his body would quickly thin and his face conceal with a beard. To everybody he would appear as a beggar on the roads and very quickly die the same.

He cupped his hands over the small black fire and pulled at a piece of green weed. Its saltiness irritated the back of his throat and he needed fresh water to drink. Running onto the wide flat beach was a shallow stream that he stopped with his foot taking great care not to get wet and therefore even colder. He stooped and then drank from the stream as he tried to evade the temporary dam spilling past his feet. Grains of sand moved in circles with the current behind the obstruction and then were quickly freed to cross the beach on their way. Attius' empty steps filled with water. In the distance the winter sky lit the hills like jewels before a heavy sky. Behind them lay the flatter richer lands that Attius hoped would contain few if any soldiers and it was this hideaway that he had to aim for. It was unlikely that an army would be raised against him for without incrimination in Macrius' plot he was just a deserter. Instead arrest and persecution would arrive in the guise of an agent sent to find him. It was now down to Attius to avoid making mistakes in this strange territory, its people unlike his own and the roads unlike the ones that he had known at home. In his practical way Longinus would have known what to do but he was dead and Attius was regretful that he hadn't revealed to the fisherman the whereabouts of the body so that he may have had a burial of sorts. In his heart he feared the shadow of Longinus' ghost following him, unable ever to placate it with offerings of food for its journey through the afterlife where it would remain to forever torment him. The struggle now though was for the living and after taking one last look along the beach, Attius turned inland.

Nothing grew in the hedges that he could eat; there were no berries or fruits of any kind to be had. Small animals that he tried to catch, easily ran away. Ceres was keeping her rich larder closed until Summer when fruits would be at hand and for the taking by all. Until then Attius would have to watch the land sleeping and, not being a slave, he would find it difficult offering himself for work without arousing suspicion. He possessed few skills, if any, not remaining in the army long enough to have developed them. Walking without direction he eventually stumbled across a road, begged himself the smallest of coins and asked as to his whereabouts.

'Aquae Sulis is close,' said the old lady. 'We're going to be healed.' She smiled kindly clutching the elbow of her husband. 'Now, out of our way if you will. I've given you coinage,' and Attius moved aside to let them pass. 'Aquae Sulis,' he thought. He had been there and might be able to remember the roads home although a few years since. Walking across the road he gently held his hand out to stop a wagon slowly rumbling its way towards him.

'Please, have you come from Aquae Sulis?' he asked.

'I have.' came the reply.

'I ask for news, not money. Is there fresh news?'

'News of what?' the disgruntled farmer replied. 'What news could concern you? Now out of my way!' And he cracked his whip for an increase in speed from the idling beast.

Attius couldn't have known it but the arrow meant for Valerius had missed its target. It had also missed Sisenna but had found lodgings in the guts of another centurion. That was murder and more seriously an attempt upon the life of the governor himself. News ought to have spread like wildfire from the settlements outside Isca and merchants using these roads in all weathers would have aided its spread to all corners of the province. Who was potentially to blame? The whispers would upset a province at peace and Attius hoped that the fingers were being pointed unfairly at others – namely the Silures. Yet they had been pacified and had accepted their peace; so there had to be other reasons at work. The agents were tasked to secretly find out why.

With the few bronze coins safely in his hand and the prospect of a better meal at the nearest market, Attius grew a little in strength and hope that he would survive. With impunity he shouted after the farmer and his cart 'Lindinis?'

'Thirty miles or so,' came the reply and Attius plodded after it.

It was a while before food was found and he pushed it into his weather worn face. The coins hadn't bought a feast and not wishing to stay there too long, Attius attached himself to whomever or whatever was travelling his way, a loaf of bread in his bag. The stall keeper had suggested that his coins were forgeries and Attius not wanting to argue politely pointed out that he could not be responsible for the kindness that came his way and neither would he be giving the coins back! A coin was a coin good or bad. A milestone indicated a change in direction for Sorviodunum at the crossroads, yet Attius, fearful at going in the wrong direction, ignored it as he had never heard his father speak of the place and therefore had little reason to go there himself. Why turn from a perfectly good road that is taking you where you wish to be and this one offered the predictability of reaching Lindinis sometime at the end of the far horizon. The ill discipline of the beggar was beginning to suit and Attius trudged on. Occasionally a soldier would pass him by, usually an officer returning to the comforts of his villa estate lying sheltered somewhere in a valley and no doubt close to the road. Attius would forget his military bearing and keep his head low thus avoiding recognition. With the loaf of bread soon gone and little in the way of willing donors to provide for more, his strength again began to waver. He had no thoughts for who exactly it was that would be waiting at Lindinis to meet him and wondered why somebody would help him without the company of their very own son. They hadn't met Attius. What could he tell them about the folly of their son and were they even still alive? Along with his doubts resurfaced the hunger and for the first time he genuinely feared for his own life, as useless as it was proving to be.

Lying back he slumped on the verge, his sandals long past being useful, his tunic a myriad of smells and stains and his beard itching in the heat of the day. He watched, as in the distance, people were leaving the road in small groups and then returning a little later. This indicated a potential richness in pickings and, like the opportunist wolf, he pulled himself up and made off in their direction. It didn't take him long to leave the road and begin the gentle serene walk up the slope and towards the temple which had been set in its own grounds. Attius nodded to the party just leaving and before entering stood back to admire the building. Its simplicity shone through, designed with smooth whitewashed walls under a brown tiled roof. An open door invited him to go in and there inside stood the effigy of the god or goddess of that place decked in the greenery of the hedges and smelling sweet with the numerous bouquets spread at its base. The air was both still and cool compared to the heat outside and briefly Attius found a moment to think. A stone trough served by a spring offered worshippers a drink from the bronze ladle chained to it. Attius quickly looked around before picking amongst the flowers. Where were the coins? There had to be some. A few emerged from the petals along with other trinkets of devotion although he was pleased not to have touched a curse tablet if one were even there. Instead he took what he could use before replacing the flower display beneath the watching god. Composing himself Attius then drank from the trough and left. Only the priests in their white robes standing at the edge of the clearing saw him go.

Realising that the road lacked opportunity for profit, he turned from it and headed once more for the woods, thinking that where one temple stood there had to be others. So far he had been lucky – unopposed and unchallenged – and came to the conclusion that Lindinis would be the wrong move, if not full of danger. Macrius' family like his own were probably under arrest and it was his own mother that he really cared for. He needed to change direction and head east, getting home if not only for her. In the dappled light of the trees and whilst idly weighing up his options, Attius admired the work of the woodman with his neatly sawn and stacked pile of logs. Had he trespassed onto a villa estate? As the afternoon sun turned its back upon mankind, tiredness overcame him and very soon Attius was asleep. It was to be a rekindling of a fire close by that awoke him.

Laughter echoed through the woods along with the shouting that accompanied it. In his lonely separated world, Attius had forgotten what it was to work together and through the thinnest of coppicing he watched carefully as silhouettes moved around the fires. Still with tired eyes it was difficult to see exactly how many men were at work and what they were doing, yet they came and went from the darkness with bundles of wood in their arms. One by one faint orange glows would burst into life and the wood smoke drift through the forest before spinning, caught in the breeze. The glow would soon disappear although the smell of hot fires remained and Attius, bag clutched tightly in his hand was ready for another escape. The rich aroma of cooking meats stopped him. With the workmen temporarily away gathering more wood, he took the opportunity of snaking forward in the grass to see what was going on. Before him there had been built five or more shelters that he could make out, with their own wicker fences for warmth and protection. Inside these and unlike anything he had ever seen before in his life, great mounds of earth exhaled tongues of fire, the blues and yellows indicating a fierce heat. A figure gently opened one of the ports on the side of the mound with an iron rod and looked inside. He closed it quickly and then returned to the front where he pushed another length of wood into the stoke hole and stood back. Immediately flashes from the dome lit the structure before dying back. Again he returned to look into the port hole, only this time he took a bronze rod hanging nearby and dipped it into the glowing liquid inside. Withdrawing it quickly the molten glass clung to the rod and Attius watched silently from his hiding place as the workman blew the orange orb into a larger shape before gently spinning it about him. Several times he did this, before rolling the rod on a flat bench and smoothing the hot glass in a wet piece of leather. Eventually he snapped it free of its mouthpiece by tapping it whereupon the glass vessel fell gently into the cooling embers of another oven close at hand. Many times he did this before his audience quietly hiding in the woods.

With the night growing on and getting colder, the tired workers stopped their laughter and slowed right down in their labours too. They would all need to eat soon before the dawn called them to their beds and the fires be allowed to safely die down. Feeling as hungry as they were, Attius saw his chance and crawled out from his hiding place and towards the direction of the food. There on an iron griddle were the sausages cooling nicely in the crisp fresh air that always seems to arrive before dawn. He quickly snatched one up and tasted the dry but slightly moist meat in his mouth and ate without stopping. There were plenty there to be had and he greedily stole another. Without shadow for a warning an iron studded boot came down hard upon his wrist pinning it to the warm earth.

'What have we caught here? A woodland thief?'

Attius looked in desperation at his foolishness. He had come so far without detection and now this. What was he to say for being there?

'Please, I have travelled a long way without stopping and I am very hungry. I haven't eaten meat for a long time and the smell of your cooking woke me. I have been sleeping in the woods,' and he pointed behind him as if they were to care. 'I'm sorry. Had I the money then I would pay you.'

'Are you alone?' his captor asked.

'Yes.' Attius answered. 'I'm looking for a friend of mine. He told me that his family were from here and that we would meet up again. Gaius Macrius Sulla. Do you know him?'

'No,' came the reply at a time when Attius feared that he had said too much.

'I may know him,' said a voice emerging from the dancing shadows. 'What reasons have you to meet up?'

Along with the work Attius was now very aware that the laughter had stopped too and that he was the sole interest of conversation. The few workers that were there that morning gathered closer to see what was happening to their captive amongst the furnaces spitting flames into the darkness.

'You can let go of his wrist,' the new stranger said, allowing Attius to get to his feet. A quiet nod had indicated to the man behind to seize him properly whilst they tied him up but it was all too obvious even in the smoking gloom and crackling heat. Attius, snatching his bag up, swung at the man before him and he stumbled before falling to the floor over the sausages. The ashes from the griddle ignited little fires of their own, especially where the heat from the furnaces had dried the ground, and they danced like spirits in their freedom before dying out. Attius quickly made to escape by lashing out at the man directly behind him but the woodman blocked his every move by mimicking his actions against the backdrop of quiet light. One of the braver then swung at Attius with a hot bronze rod, the warm metal eating into the softness of his face. Attius screamed.

'You, bastard!' he shouted and the man backed away before the murderous agent came forward again. 'Get him men,' he repeated. 'Get him.' Attius this time withdrew his sword from his bag and snatched the blade clean from its scabbard; with the weight of his opponent clumsily falling upon the narrowest of sword points, it easily tore into his stomach and brought him down. Attius looked at the man lying at his feet and remembered seeing every hair on his head as he fell moaning and dying before him. This was the first man that he had ever killed and he started to shake, staring at the body there. Without any time for thought, he threatened the remaining workers who one by one ran away, leaving Attius alone. Under the rising sun with all the wooden structures empty, the fires burning down quietly without man's control and the glass-makers all gone, Attius was truly on the run.

The sweetest of dew upon a clod of earth helped to quell the immediate pain and given a little time, the wound eventually closed its pink lips to form a slightly raised scar that he picked at. Attius was now marked out and witnesses to that night's trouble would be able to instantly recognise him. The dead man's blood though was little more that a brown stain upon his tunic as a reminder of the killing. Now possessed of nothing but fear, he stumbled over the roughest of ground trying to make for the higher land where he could hide. There were no milestones there and fewer people either to point the way or offer aid. He could have simply died and nobody known, except for the putrid smell of a rotting carcass coming from the scented meadows. A warm breeze instead blew into his face and lifted his matted hair. He was sweating and with a dry throat needed more and more to drink. However the summer rains were quickly evaporated from any puddles on the chalk ridge, with water becoming scarce. Fearing the valley bottoms, he decided against venturing too close to farmsteads for fear of being seen and made do instead with picking at the darkest of green grasses and chewing them over for their moisture before spitting them out. He washed his face in a similar fashion to cool it and then lay down to sleep in the warmest of nature's beds.

The low clouds coming from the east were there when he woke, almost serving as a pointer towards home. That was now his plan; to get there no matter what. With berries now on their bushes, wild apples and fruit, and occasionally the smallest of shrimps allowed to fall through his fingers with the silt of the river, he kept himself alive. Without detection, his spirits rose and even the loneliest shepherd with his dogs would acknowledge him from afar. In meeting another gravelled road he avoided it except to hurry out and read its milestone. SORVIODUNUM two thousand paces. Attius didn't know where Sorviodunum was and retreated quickly off the road. In avoiding the small market that had established itself at the crossroads upon the hill, he crossed the open fields at night thus bypassing the settlement with the barking of guard dogs that could have led to his capture. The road east continued and in the moonlight he could make out by tracing his fingers in the shadow the word CALLEVA. Still keeping at a safe distance from the road, he decided to follow its course as it led east and towards home. Eventually after a day and a half's slow travelling this road too emerged at a settlement of scattered buildings where people busied themselves in their everyday lives. He decided to risk entering as a vagrant, in the quest for news carried by merchants and their wagons, and also to see if there was the opportunity of stealing more food. The usual array of open fronted shops greeted him with the produce swinging from iron hooks – a chicken, a piglet and pieces of salted lamb. A tavern with the smell of ale wafting in the warm thunderous air echoed with talk from its dark interior. He looked at the eggs lying in their straw bed at the bottom of the roughest bowl and the soft fruits for sale alongside them but it was something else that had caught his eye. In large carved letters at the junction of the road was painted the word DUROCORNOVIUM. That was the way home.

Without wanting to stop, Attius drew his cloak across his head feigning the need for shade, firstly from the sun and then from the inevitable storm that was closely following behind. He tried to use his toes to grip his flaying sandals that had now broken free from their leather thongs. The shoes themselves, missing many of their original hobnails, were making walking on the most even of surfaces difficult but the road wasn't at all broken and was in a good state of repair. However his feet twisted and lurched at every landing in their attempt at moving that little bit faster. This wasn't an orderly military march – it was a retreat and one into which Attius was drawing attention to himself. He despised the jeering crowd at the tavern, trying to avoid the pebbles thrown at him and without tripping over his precarious feet, stumbled on, cursing them all. He was glad to be free of civilization and on the open road where his mishaps could follow closely like the fading evening shadows. Rain was coming and Attius veered away for shelter. A small group of mounted soldiers passed by splashing though the puddles and with their heads turned away from the direction of the rain they barely noticed him. He recognised them as auxiliaries on routine patrol and knew that they would soon be gone, wishing to get in out the rain themselves. However they had many miles to travel before that. They sped up and gave him little thought as they passed by, spears, shields and swords at their sides. Fortuna smiled on in her favours.

The sound of the two stones grinding against each other pleased him for although they were only flint they ground the damp ears of corn into a floury paste that he could simply heat up and eat. The constant need for food was making him delirious and, only eating when his body craved it, had deprived him of all social order. The wheat heads that he had stolen were golden and full yesterday but were now heavy with rain and were proving of little value in keeping him going. Attius remembered Gaius Helvius Bonus clapping his hands at the expectation of the next course to arrive at his table and then lustily devouring it. His stomach cried out to be at that very table now. In the privacy of his hideaway he could lapse into semi consciousness, with a thousand stains on his clothes, a beard and a broken body, and listen for the faint call from the imaginary slaves to say that the bath house was now hot and ready for use. He could see the fruit orchard bursting with its wealth and watch others as they toiled in the fields in order to fill the larder. The Penates, what use were they to him now? Lying in the roots of a tree and temporarily oblivious to the sound of the rain, Attius stared at the ground before him poking at it with the rust pitted blade of his father's sword.

Across the low ridge on the southern sky he saw a figure riding towards him at some speed in the gathering dusk of a wet evening. Was this to be his captor? Keeping low, Attius pushed aside the tallest of the grasses that were blocking his view and watched as the lone horseman came on. Where were the others? Sensing that speed brought with it news, he feared Macrius Sulla had been caught or that war had flared up unnecessarily in the west. He quickly thought about the dead agent and the jeering crowd at the tavern and his heart beat faster. Was capture imminent? The renewed danger roused him.

The cavalry mask fitted him well. He had tried it on many times before, although unaware of what it actually looked like. Its silver face reflected his own distorted image every time he admired it or used it to pick at the scab of his wound. Attius tied it securely around his neck and stood up. Through its narrow eye slits he watched as the approaching rider pushed his tired horse up and over the incline and towards him. He crouched a little lower behind the green blinds of the tree's lower canopy clutching the sword tightly in his hand. The rider could be harmless but as he approached, Attius recognised him as being an imperial messenger on an errand. To stop any messenger was a crime. Yet Attius could scare him, to get news but perhaps also to rob him for money as well as taking his horse, which was a huge risk. Time stopped and he was there.

Between the ears of the horse its rider saw a man emerge from the edge of the road, from where a tired horse hadn't sensed there being any danger. Nobody expected an attack upon the imperial post and especially in a part of the island where peace had reigned for eighty years or so. What was its purpose? Attius ran out wearing the mask and shouting through his skin of silver causing the horse to swerve in an attempt at avoiding him. White bubbles of sweaty foam had mixed with the rain on its coat and in avoiding being caught, it reared up. The rider too without drawing his sword kicked out at the assailant before him and his boots thumped into Attius' unprotected chest. Still Attius persevered, managing to snatch one rein in his hand. He had hold of the horse but as it spun around the rider looked down and again lashed out with his boot. Attius, sword in hand pushed against the rider's leg forcing him to topple from the saddle. He fell on his back against the unforgiving surface below, the neck guard of his helmet folding up in the fall. He lay there with his face twisted towards the wet dirt, blood slowly oozing from his lips, eyes closed and barely breathing. The horse, in sudden renewed fear bolted forcing Attius to let it go. He hadn't wanted that, as its capture further along the road would alarm others as to its rider's fate. He watched it barely get away before the flaying reins became entangled in its front legs causing it to stumble and fall. Apparently only winded it lay across the road. After a few moments Attius sensed that it had broken its shoulder and wouldn't be getting to its feet ever again. He went to the stricken animal and would do nothing for it. To have cut his throat and save it suffering was too obvious. This had to be an accident. He returned to stare at the rider. Around his shoulder was the bag of the imperial post, inside it news. Attius poked at the man on the floor trying to elicit a response but none came. He too was close to death. Attius picked carefully at the satchel, opening the flap, and then withdrew the various rolls inside. He looked around before removing his mask and then with shaking hands he began to break the seals on the parchment quickly reading them before coming to the one that caused him to shake violently. In uncomplicated Latin and with rain drops gently falling upon it, it read:

· TO THE GOVERNOR AND LEGATES OF II AVG · XX
VALERIA VICTRIX · VI VICTRIX · CAESAR HADRIANUS
IS DEAD · PEACE TO THE CITIZENS OF BRITANNIA
AND WEALTH AND GLORY TO THE ARMIES OF ROME

Attius shook at the news not meant for his reading. He had had no right to intercept it and tried hard to put the scrolls back into their bag. His actions would not bring the empire down and the province would not fall because of his personal beliefs either. Unbeknown to him, the new Emperor Antoninus, would within two short years have called the legions from their forts and ushered them through the open wooden gates into the tribal lands of the Selgovae, Votadini and Dumnonii where, in his name, they would win a victory in Britannia. The stone wall of Hadrian would stand quietly still and be superseded by another, built further north and this time in less-permanent turf.

At the Senate of Rome, conquest was still a word used to protect the Roman way of life and that included the wealthy taking their pick of riches from the remote province of Britannia lying quietly behind its walls. On the other side barbarians looked in, and from their mountain hovels bided their time carefully for that greed to turn in upon itself before they, like Attius, and others coming after him, would strike back with a vengeance at their exclusion from the empire and her luxuries.

Without wanting to look back on that history and with a scroll in his hand, Attius, the deserter, ran off into his uncertain future.

GLOSSARY

AGGER — The raised central portion of a Roman road sloping away towards its ditches on either side.

AQUAE SULIS — Bath

ALABUM — Llandovery

AQUILA — Eagle

ANTONINUS — Roman Emperor from AD 138–161. Responsible for the re-occupation of Caledonia and for building the wall that bears his name, some 40 Roman miles long (60km) stretching from the Firth of Clyde to the Firth of Forth. Built about AD 143 in turf. Antoninus was what history refers to as the fourth of the so called five 'good' emperors.

AENEAS — The legendary founder of Rome having escaped the perils following the sack of Troy.

APOLLO — God of music, poetry and healing

CENTURION — A career soldier who had been promoted to the rank. They often led by example and had worked their way up. In charge of 80 men, there were 60 centurions in a legion.

CORONA AUREA — An award for bravery given to Centurions and above. A golden crown.

CICIUM — Y Gaer

CALLEVA — Calleva Atrebatum translates as the City of the Atrebates in the wood. Silchester (Hants).

CORINIUM — Corinium Dubunnorum. Cirencester (Glos). After Londinium, it was the second largest town in Roman Britain.

CHARON — The ragged, filthy boatman who rowed the dead across the River Styx to Hades. To pay him it was customary to place a coin in the eye of the deceased. Only the bravest would be rowed across first.

CORNICEN	Horn player in the army
CERES	Mother Goddess of the Earth
DIANA	Twin sister of Apollo, she was a hunter and vindictive too. Associated with the moon as Apollo was the sun.
D M	'Dis Manibus' translating as to the spirits of the departed.
DUROTRIGIA	The land of the Durotriges – namely Dorset & Somerset.
DEVA	Chester
DUROCORNOVIUM	Wanborough (Wilts)
DENARIUS	Roman silver coin. There were 25 Denarii to the Aureus (gold coin) and 4 sestersi (bronze) to the Denarius. Common coin of payment to the army when in plentiful supply.
DONATIVE	A gift made by the new emperor to his troops. It bought their loyalty and could be either money or land.
EBORACUM	York
FORTUNA	The goddess of chance
FLORA	Goddess of flowers and blossom
GLEVUM	Gloucester
GROMA	Roman surveying instrument relying upon the use of right angles for accuracy.
GLADIUS	Ubiquitous Roman short stabbing sword. Like most Roman arms it was adapted from elsewhere (Spain).
GOBANNIUM	Abergavenny
HADRIAN	Roman emperor from AD 117–138. Visited Britain and instigated the building of the wall in his name to separate the barbarians from the empire. Begun in roughly AD 122 and taking six years, it ran from coast to coast and was 80 Roman miles long (117km). Hadrian was the third of the five 'good' emperors.

HARUSPEX	Roman priest who divine d the future from the entrails of sacrifice animals.
HASTA	Cavalry spear
H S E	'Hic Situs Est' translates as 'Here he lies.'
ISCA	Isca Silurum (Carleon, South Wales) Isca Dumnoniorum (Exeter)
JANUS	The Roman god of doorways and beginnings had two faces – one that looked backwards and one that looked forwards. The first hour of the day was sacred to him.
JUPITER	God of the sky and daylight. Had the power over thunder and lightning and all weather. Regarded as the supreme being in the heavens.
LINDUM	Lincoln
LONDINIUM	London
LEUCOMAGUS	East Anton, Andover (Hants)
LARES	Deified spirits of dead family members. It was important not to rouse them to anger. Worshipped at a small family shrine in the house with offerings of wine or incense.
LUGUDUNUM	Lyon (France)
LICIUM	Roman underpants
LEGIO II AUGUSTA	One of the original four legions to have invaded Britain in AD 43. It found its permanent base at Carleon in South Wales.
LEGIO XX	Correctly known as Valeria Victrix. Again thought to be one of the original four legions to have landed in AD 43. Instrumental in crushing Boudicca's revolt and found its permanent base at Chester.
LEGIO VI VICTRIX	Brought over by Hadrian in AD 122 to replace the 'lost' IX Hispannia. Found its permanent base in York.
LUENTINUM	Pumsaint
LINDINIS	Ilchester (Somerset)

MANSIO	Roman overnight stabling and accommodation block.
MORIDUNUM	Carmarthen
MERCURY	Winged messenger of Jupiter. He protected merchants and travellers alike.
MEDICUS	Roman medical orderly in the field
MILITES INTENDE	'Soldiers, fall in!'
MARS ULTOR	Mars was the god of war and earlier the god too of protection from crop disease. Mars Ultor is Mars the Avenger.
MAGISTER EQUITUM	Master of the horse. Commander
MINERVA	Goddess of intellectual and academic activity and also goddess of healing.
NEPTUNE	God of the sea who could calm the waves.
OPTIO	Second in command of a century. Would be the Centurion's natural successor.
OCEANUS	The great river that the Romans believed encircled the flat earth and marked their known limits.
P MUMMIUS SISENNA	Roman governor of Britannia AD 133–135 or later. The usual term of office was five years. Superseded by Quintus Lollius Urbicus upon Hadrian's death in AD 138.
PARENTALIA	A feast of the dead, especially the parents, when relatives would gather to sprinkle food on the grave of the deceased in order to feed them and stop them looking for food themselves. Held mid February.
PRINCIPIA	The legionary headquarters building.
PRAEFECTUS	Praefectus Castrorum was the prefect of the camp but not the Legate himself. The Legate ran the Legion, the Praefectus the camp.
PROBATIO	Translates as 'probation' in English and was the time that the army had to evaluate their new recruits. Usually 3–4 months.

PAPILIO	Roman soldiers thought that their leather tents when rolled up resembled the lava of grubs. Translates as 'moth'.
PENATES	Were the gods of the larder and critical in ensuring that people had enough food to eat.
PICTS	'Painted People'. Barbarians from beyond the northern wall.
PLUTO	King of the Dead
ROME	Fabled to last for 1200 years. Founded 753 BC and fell AD 476.
SILVANUS	The old god of sacred woods
SOL	The sun
SATURNALIA	Feast in December to celebrate the death of the old god Saturn and his subsequent rebirth. Slaves were given the freedom and privileges of their masters for the duration of the festivities.
STRIGIL	Curved bronze bathing implement used for scraping the dirt out of the skin after a hot steam.
SESTERTIUS	See DENARIUS
SALVETE	A greeting or salute
SABRINA FLUVIUS	The River Severn estuary
SAMIAN	High quality ceramic tableware notably red in colour with relief decoration, usually imported from Gaul.
SACELLUM	The shrine in a fort where the standards and pay chests were securely locked away.
LORICA SEGMENTATA	Roman armour made of interlinking metal plates that could offer excellent protection.
SILURIA	Home of the Silures, the tribe that occupied southern and mid Wales and who gave the Roman armies many years of intense, bitter fighting.
SELGOVAE	Tribal group of southern Scotland along with the Dumnonii and Votadini

SORVIODUNUM	Small market settlement outside Salisbury (Wilts)
STYX	River of the Underworld running between swampy marshland and over which Charon rowed the dead. The living could never cross.
TURMA	A cavalry squadron of 32 men
TARTARUS	The furthest part of the underworld. Hell where the burning river Phlegothon ran as opposed to the river Lethe that ran towards Elysium. The godless inhabited Tartarus.
TESSARIUS	Roman military official
VENTA SILURUM	Market place of the Silures. Caerwent
VENTA BELGARUM	Market place of the Belgae. Winchester
VICUS	The shanty town of dwellings that always grew up around the boundaries of Roman forts.
VEXILLATION	A smaller unit of the Roman legion where the full force is not required. Usually 1000 men.
VEXILLUM	Roman flag or standard
VESTA	Roman god of the hearth and one in which there was no bodily image made. Symbolic of the eternal power of Rome. If a scrap of food was offered during a meal to the flames then it was good luck if it burst into life and did not smoulder.
VERULAMIUM	St Albans
VIRGIL	Roman poet in the early years of the Empire following the civil wars of Octavian (Augustus). Virgil bestowed upon the Roman people 'Empire without Limit'. Rome felt that she had the moral right to conquer and to pay for that conquest there had to be a reward – the wages of victory.